LUISA
AND
THE
SILENCE

Claudio Piersanti

*Translated from
the Italian
by George Hochfield*

ᵀMᴾ

THE MARLBORO PRESS/NORTHWESTERN

Northwestern University Press   *Evanston, Illinois*

LUISA

AND

THE

SILENCE

The Marlboro Press/Northwestern
Northwestern University Press
Evanston, Illinois 60208-4210

Originally published in Italian under the title
Luisa e il Silenzio. Copyright © 1997
by Giangiacomo Feltrinelli Editore, Milano.
English translation copyright © 2002
by the Marlboro Press/Northwestern.
Published 2002. All rights reserved.

Printed in the United States of America

10 9 8 7 6 5 4 3 2 1

ISBN 0-8101-6088-9 (cloth)
ISBN 0-8101-6080-3 (paper)

Library of Congress
Cataloging-in-Publication Data

Piersanti, Claudio.
  [Luisa e il silenzio. English]
  Luisa and the silence / Claudio Piersanti ;
translated from the Italian by George Hochfield.
      p. cm.
  ISBN 0-8101-6088-9 (cloth : alk. paper) —
ISBN 0-8101-6080-3 (pbk. : alk. paper)
  I. Hochfield, George. II. Title.
  PQ4876.I3295 L8513 2001
  853'.914—dc21

                              2001005118

La nuit est une grande cité endormie
où le vent souffle . . .

—Philippe Jaccottet

LUISA
AND
THE
SILENCE

1

WHEN THE RADIO ALARM SOUNDED, SHE WAS
dreaming of a long stairway suspended in the void.
It was exactly six o'clock. Luisa opened her eyes
and for a few seconds continued to see the stairway
that she had been climbing for hours. It was the inside stairway of a building without walls or floors,
where beds, bathrooms, and kitchens swayed over a
black abyss. All the apartments were inhabited, and
life was going on almost normally. She remembered clearly the annoyed expression of a mother
continually calling to her three children, who were
happily scampering like monkeys from one beam
to another. Keep still, she repeated like a refrain, or
you'll fall down, keep still! An absurd dream, full of
dizziness and already forgotten complications, but
not at all unpleasant. She lived there with someone,
in the vertiginous building. But with whom? He
wore mirrored sunglasses like Renata's; she remembered nothing else.

She turned on the light and hurriedly put on

her woolen bathrobe. It was pitch dark outside and the air smelled of frost. The radiators wouldn't come on until six-thirty, too late for her on the fourth floor. The tenants in the garret complained that their apartments did not warm up until nine o'clock. The usual inconveniences of old central heating systems. Luckily, it only took the electric heaters five minutes to make the bathroom and kitchen usable.

She went to make some coffee and turned on the radio. Then she took the cloth from the canary's cage and waited for the first heat from the bluish flame under the coffeepot, which certainly did not warm her but kept her company. From the small kitchen window she could see a long stretch of the avenue lighted by overhanging lamps, the already open newsstand surrounded by bundles of papers still untied, and part of the entrance to the bar. Great halos of nighttime humidity had formed around the lights, and on the sidewalks large streaks of ice had appeared that the muffled up passersby carefully avoided. There were a great many people who rose earlier than she, so she couldn't complain. Besides, it was Walter's turn this week, and she didn't have to take her car out of the garage. Even if he was driving, she still felt the need to check on the density of the fog. Moving close to the window, she managed to make out clearly enough the bare branches of the chestnut trees rising above the gates of the park. A light fog for the season.

The coffee came up with its usual cheerful gurgling, and as she poured it the radio news began. Her mother used to say that the first hour after getting up was the best one of the day, and she was right. Luisa had experimented when she was young; study during that hour was worth a whole afternoon. She ate four *biscotti,* emptied the cup, and lit her first Multifilter. The pack that was newly opened would last her exactly two days, at least if no one in the office forgot to buy some. The news this morning was bad: at least two wars, and the usual terrible road accidents. At the end of the newscast, after a loud musical theme that she liked, they interviewed an Italian actor who had had a success in America and spoke from Los Angeles by telephone. What did it really mean in a man's life to go for a stroll in Los Angeles, ascend to a suite on the hundredth floor, look down on the lighted city at his feet, and think that on all the television sets in all those houses his handsome, cheerful countenance often appeared? Only to a few, and they are very few, does an extraordinary life come; all the others must be satisfied with what they have. Luisa did not suffer from envy; she never had. There were many causes of suffering she had not been spared, but she did not think herself more unfortunate than others. She had her radio, her cigarette, and a pleasant warmth began to spread around her. There was no reason to foresee that today would be different from other days.

With her bathrobe finally open over men's pajamas, her radio under her arm, and a cigarette in her mouth, she went humming to the shower. The bathroom was small, and the electric heater warmed it perfectly. She was surprised every morning at the change from intense cold when she first got up to the moment of the shower. She got out of bed convinced that she would have to avoid it, and instead she always did it gladly. A brief shower of barely five minutes that nevertheless was her official entry to the day. After the shower, she combed her hair and put on her makeup quickly, with a few automatic gestures. She concentrated only on the line made with her lipstick that had to follow the shape of her lips exactly. She was proud of her well-formed mouth, exactly comparable to her mother's beautiful one. For the rest, she didn't consider herself either beautiful or ugly, and growing old had not changed her much. She was sixty, but when she was looking her best she didn't show it. The only real sign of age was an oblong mole that had grown in recent months near her collarbone. She had seen others like it often, and much more disfiguring, on the noses and faces of people of a certain age. At least she could hide hers.

She chose something to wear without much thought and began to get dressed. Her clothes were all quite elegant and always well pressed, even if she hid them under a smock at work. During the early years she hated that blue smock, perhaps because only the clerks and warehouse people had to wear it, the lowest levels of the company. Then she had begun to appreciate it, partly for its ample pockets, and partly because it protected her clothing. Now that she was no longer obliged to wear it, she found it elegant. She had gotten into the habit of keeping the collar a little raised, and when she walked through the halls, she thrust her hands into the pockets of her smock and toyed with her cigarettes and lighter. She imagined herself walking like that, and she felt the desire to be in her office already, remembering all the tasks she had left unfinished and the list of those that awaited her in the afternoon. None was special; it was a slack time. She ought to hurry if she wanted to drink a cappuccino at the bar. Finished dressing, she took another quick look at herself in the mirror and decided to put on her fur, even though she no longer liked how it looked. She put on her wool hat and gloves in the elevator; the folding umbrella had refused to fit completely inside her bag, and she decided not to bother with it.

As usual, she was the first one to leave her building. The cold immediately froze her face and legs, and a thousand minute drops of icy fog collected on the lenses of her glasses. She crossed the avenue and quickly entered the bar. There were seven or eight people who seemed many more because of their enormous down jackets and sheepskin coats. She wiped her glasses with a paper napkin and drank her warm cappuccino all in one draft.

"I'm going to be late," she said to the barman, who answered with the usual cautions about haste.

She was not really late; she had a mania about punctuality and knew that Walter would have trouble at the intersection where they were supposed to meet. The police hardly allowed him to stop long enough for her to get in the car, and if they were in a bad mood, they blew their whistles furiously and, white phosphorescent gloves in the air, waved them on pitilessly, as if that intersection was their own home!

For years she had walked the same length of street, but each time she found it less short than she remembered it. She began walking slowly and then, without noticing it, lengthened her pace and arrived at the traffic light almost at a run, out of breath and her calves aching. At the light, where her avenue crossed a wider one, there was a certain animation: some pedestrians with briefcases and valises stamped their feet and stared at the stop sign as if it were an enemy. Walter had not yet arrived; it was a quarter past seven, and he was in danger of being late.

A girl in a fur jacket and black miniskirt was washing the still dark windows of a bank. She wasn't pretty, but the men were giving her long, covetous looks all the same. Two youths even made a risqué remark. Men understand nothing of feminine beauty; when they're young, they see the prettiest ones only accidentally. They have delightful girls in their classes, and they nudge one another like idiots when they see two crooked legs covered with net stockings.

Walter was not to be seen. Yet there wasn't much traffic. The buses, dirty with fine bits of mud up to their windows, were crowded with hundreds of people being carried to the industrial suburbs, and just at that point in the road they speeded up in order to get into the center lane. There was only one policeman, the tall one with the stern face, but he was taking it easy on his corner, lazily operating the push buttons for the traffic lights.

At seven twenty-five Luisa began to be worried. Another minute and they would surely be late. She was cut off here, with her car locked in the garage not more than two hundred meters away. She decided to go back, but her legs would not obey her; in fact, her bearing became more calm, not permitting the least anxiety, the least desire for a place other than the one she was in, to show themselves. The same proud temperament as her mother.

Walter arrived at seven twenty-eight. They looked at one another across the crosswalk that separated them, and she understood immediately what had happened when Walter indicated the miserable face of Giancarlo, late for the third time in a month. When Annarita still went with them, it was most often she who was the cause of their being late. Luckily, she had decided to go by herself, at least in winter.

When they opened the door for her, and Giancarlo, contorting himself, pulled his seat backward to allow her to get in quickly, Luisa thought that this was her family, the people she saw most and knew best: Walter, her colleague for twenty years, Giancarlo, Renata, maybe Annarita. She was not angry about their lateness, at bottom minimal; in fact, she laughed because Giancarlo played the buffoon and confessed to being a shit, and said he wanted to cut his veins or to retire. Giancarlo was a handsome young fellow of twenty-six. Even though he was blond, he had a bristly, tough beard like a black's, which contrasted with the delicate lineaments of his face. He shaved three times a week, and he had done so this morning. His too-strong aftershave aroused the usual protests from Luisa, who pretended to want the windows open a little. They exchanged witticisms about the frivolousness of men and women until they were out of the city. There was already traffic on the bypass, especially in the direction opposite to theirs, where a long trail of headlights waited, resigned and motionless in total silence, while thin clouds of fog rose from the surrounding country and shrouded the highway lights.

"Oh, what a treat!" exclaimed Walter, and without having to ask permission he turned on the radio tuned to a local station that broadcast restful music, excellent for driving or as unobtrusive background to domestic chores. Usually they did not talk during the quarter hour they spent on the bypass; the driving was more demanding, and rare comments concerned the traffic, which grew heavier as they went on. A stupid collision, or one of those inexplicable jams at their exit, which was the last one before the intercity freeway, could cost them hours of salary and ill humor. For that reason, too, they did not talk. They scanned anxiously the course of every slowdown and drew a sigh of relief when the car picked up speed. Sometimes Giancarlo took out a stopwatch he had received as a birthday present and amused himself by keeping time. On that day, with little traffic and little fog, they left the bypass after fourteen minutes and ten seconds. At the bottom of the ramp the light was green, so they could turn at high speed into the narrow street along the canal, a shortcut that made it possible to save at least five minutes. At a certain point they had to go through a little village of few houses, with a tiny square around an ugly cement fountain, and a traffic light that Walter detested.

Luisa's eye caught an open window and a bald or completely shaved man with arms crossed and a cigarette in his mouth looking out at the panorama of shrubs and grayish fog. He couldn't have been more than forty, and he appeared extremely handsome to her. Maybe he was a singer with some modern group who had just finished performing in a club near the university and was about to get some sleep.

9

Walter and Giancarlo had started to talk about football and kept it up as far as the factory.

They stamped their time cards at seven-fifty. The main entrance for visitors and managers was still locked. The red carpet on the stairway was pretentious and completely out of place. Luisa surveyed it every morning with profound disgust. Theirs had been a more than decent factory without that stupid red carpet which humiliated her. The old man didn't understand; he enjoyed too much climbing his steps imperially. It hurt her for the old fellow; perhaps he wasn't good natured, but he could boast of never having fired one of his workers. The oldest were long since retired. What was so terrible about his liking to climb the steps with his chest stuck out like an admiral? He was old, and his life could be called successful. In the dressing room where she put on her smock, she continued to think about her boss. She remembered when he had begun to cry in front of her because his wife was being operated on, and they hadn't given him much hope. He had confided everything to her like a friend, without being ashamed of his tears; he had told her about their coming from the Veneto almost sixty years ago, about his historic decision to settle here, and also about his children and the little one they had lost. She had been unable to say anything to him, standing stiffly before him with her printouts in her arms. For an instant the emotion of that day came back to her, and she called herself stupid. In the end, the old man's wife had recovered, and she, who had lost all her family without mercy and without reprieve, was moved by a fortunate old man loaded with money. Next to the women's dressing room was the sample room. Toys and boxes lay on long shelves, drenched in a repulsive smell of plastic. In the half darkness the toys gave off an air of melancholy, and she had learned not to look at them too much: the box of Virgilio the mouse, the little stunt cars, the endless series of tiny figurines that had to be assembled, destined to go with chocolate eggs and *biscotti,* the dusty metal shelves, the stacks of puzzles, the albums of sketches, the old neon tubes. For her that room was the factory's morgue.

The latest novelty was a yellow-and-red catapult "made in Taiwan." It launched heavy rubber balls that must have been permanently lost under the furniture in thousands of houses. At Intelligent Games, Inc., they cost a thousand lire, but the end price must have come to fifteen thousand, which seemed a fraud when she thought of it; and looking at the faces of the managers, it seemed to her she was working for swindlers and therefore was one herself, since in a small way she shared in the company's profits. A hundred adults—seventy workers including drivers; seven managers; and twenty-three office workers—who lived and worked with cheap little toys, and in this way took part in the functioning of the city's economy, even that of the whole world. Where is the engine of all this, where the heart that gives energy to all these things? She had asked herself this for many years, and had never found an answer. The world, for Luisa, remained a great mystery.

She crossed the showroom with her head down and entered the office area. The sales department secretaries pretended not to see her, but she was not bothered by them, a pair of geese who passed the time doing their nails. The third door from the end of the corridor was hers; if she hurried she could avoid being seen by colleagues having coffee behind the wooden screen who would have obliged her to drink some with them.

She had been saying for years that she liked to have her coffee later, that she had already had two, but in the end she found herself with a plastic glass in hand and a forbidden cigarette in her mouth that weighed on her like a sin. At that hour she didn't want to talk; she preferred to wait until eight o'clock reading the local page of the newspaper seated in her old swivel chair. She liked to stretch her legs under the desk, lean back comfortably, and bury herself for five minutes in the news stories, in harrowing automobile accidents or bloody family quarrels. F. G., a mason, who, pistol in hand, burst into the apartment of E. N., with whom he had formerly lived, and had forced her to call her current friend... prognosis uncertain for both... robbery at the Federici jewelry store... surgical forceps recovered from the stomach of a surveyor... poor fellow, how he must have suffered. Sharp forceps in the stomach, those murderers! She felt sorry for the victims; reading united her with them; still, she had to admit that it relaxed her. She did not feel she was to blame. As she grew older she had learned to transform misfortune into a subject of conversation, as when she talked with Walter about his blood tests and the many kidney problems that afflicted him.

At exactly eight o'clock the personnel manager went by, a boy of thirty who wasn't brave enough even to look at her. His gray suit too big for him, hands clasped behind his back, an awkward air of someone timid trying to look stern. When he passed, the shipping clerk made an obscene gesture with his finger, but it made nobody laugh.

2

THIS MORNING THE DIRECTORS AND THE COM-
mendatore were having an important meeting with
the department heads, and from nine o'clock on
there was a continual coming and going of secretaries with slips of paper and trays of coffee. When
they left the door open a little, Luisa could catch
sight through her glass wall of the tired expressions
of four men in shirt sleeves, one of them with his
hands in his hair as he studied the papers in front of
him, another who stretched out his heavy ex-peas-
ant's arm and signaled no with a thick but well-
manicured finger in the direction of someone who
could not be seen, and two others talking between
themselves and certainly commenting on the secretaries, because both had their eyelids a little closed
as men do when they speak of women's rear ends.
They would remain shut in there at least until one-
thirty, then they would go to lunch in the center, to
Franco's as usual, only to return toward four a little
tight and guffawing, the old man cheerful in front

of them all, with a foul cigar and breath smelling of grappa, his son immediately behind him, called the "little professor" even though he was approaching fifty, giggling in his father's presence but underneath it all depressed. Nice life, that of an executive, not to mention salaries and extras. Convenient to stay at work until eight in the evening and return home when there was no more traffic on the bypass, especially when they could come in at ten in the morning or even later. It's those two hours that make all the difference.

The morning became steadily grayer. The fluorescent lights were on in all the rooms, and eyes were already burning. For half an hour at least, no one went by in the access road to the factories: now, at last, a muffled up messenger was arriving with a box tied to the rack of his motorbike. Luisa stared at him, seized by an unusual maternal concern for this young man who went around in the cold on wet streets just to deliver a diary or some other stupid birthday gift. Usually she didn't care for young men, but this one made her feel sympathetic. Perhaps because he was working. Luckily, one of the scoundrels from the Modern Body Repair Shop had gone out to meet him and he jumped back on his bike, which he had left running so as not to lose time. She would willingly have kept her eyes on him as far as the turnout, but she noticed that Renata had also interrupted her work at the computer and was watching her with a warm look, her mouth open in a smile she had learned as a child and which as an adult made her look a bit silly. Renata's round face had only two expressions: it could be very sad or very happy; there were no nuances. When she was happy and opened her fleshy, doll-like mouth, her bad teeth showed, ruined by the caramels she ate continually to keep herself from smoking, and so even when she laughed she didn't convey good cheer but sadness, and no one was friendly with her. Her coworkers in all departments were grateful for the many favors she did for them, but none went further than a cordial greeting through the glass on their way to the coffee machine.

"We can't do any more this morning," she said in her little girl's voice before Luisa was concentrated on her screen again.

"If we start out like that, we'll never get anywhere," Luisa answered, starting to work again. She had been brusque; after a minute she felt displeased with herself and added, "Have you already done the figures in the pink file?"

"Yes, ma'am, finished a while ago."

Luisa knew this but pretended to be surprised and declared she would offer her a coffee. They lit cigarettes, one of the two they had decided to allow themselves before lunchtime, and fell into thoughts of work and their usual reveries. In their moments of rest, Renata worried in silence about her two children, added up the homework not done for class, the bad company, the meatballs already prepared in the freezer, the shirts she had to buy on sale. Luisa's thoughts habitually did not wander far from the present, especially when she was in the office. At that moment, they actually stopped there near her, because she began to think about Renata, the only employee who depended directly upon her and whom she had just made to feel guilty. She had barely greeted her when she came in, and had become absorbed in reading the paper. She behaved with her like all the others, that is, she forgot about her, and Renata was aware of it and suffered because of it, increased her attentions, and worked harder and with greater care. At bottom, she wasn't stupid, a good heart is never stupid, and sometimes she spoke well, she was informed, she knew the musicians, the politicians, the television journalists. But she talked too much, and often with the squeaky voice of a little lady ten years old. She tried to smile, too, like a little girl, and those black teeth were the coup de grâce. Luisa ought to find a way to straighten her out; she had been thinking of it for five years, ever since Renata had been placed in her office. She would have liked to say: If you need money for the dentist, I'll lend it to you, but she knew that wasn't the problem. It was enough to look at her. She was getting fat and didn't mind, she took no care of her smock, which by now didn't fit and was mended around the buttons. She was thirty-eight and looked fifty. There she was, on her broken-down chair, her plump thighs spread like a child watching television, with that slovenliness that women sometimes allow themselves with other women.

It depends on the mother you had, Luisa thought, and she was glad to remember her own for a few minutes, forcing herself not to think of her as she had become with illness, but imagining her young and healthy with her luminous smile and the hazel eyes that shone like two crystals. Her mother had never been untidy, not even at six in the morning, not even in winter, and there weren't electric heaters then or programmable radiators, and the cold lasted at least until ten o'clock.

Little by little the numbers of her calculations occupied her thoughts and her mother slipped away. The miracle happened, as it did every day, today just a bit late. The toys were transformed into numbers that interested banks and wholesalers and merchants, store owners, salesmen, sellers of advertising space; now the numbers claimed all her attention, and Renata did not dare disturb her, no one stopped to exchange a few words, the time sped by, it vanished. This was the Luisa her coworkers knew. In an old caricature done by a switchboard operator, Luisa was portrayed in front of the computer screen, her birdlike throat stretched forward and glasses thick as the bottoms of bottles. Next to her, still in caricature, her human-looking printer churned out sheets by the kilometer, full of numbers. Sometimes the Commendatore in person stopped at her door and watched with satisfaction, because Luisa didn't even notice him.

She was a good worker, esteemed by all her colleagues for her precision and punctuality, but she did not drive herself merely to please whoever paid her salary; she worked hard in obedience to an inner command, and no signs of submissiveness or excessive respect ever escaped her even by accident. She blushed with pride when Christmas greetings were brought to her from the old man himself, and when he personally handed over the usual gift package and bonus at the end of the year. Some found her too much attached to her work, and perhaps a little cold, but only two or three who had had occasion to test her most cutting reactions ever spoke ill of her.

This morning the page of summaries kept her occupied until one o'clock; by then the columns of numbers obeyed servilely and ran in perfect order; she studied them and restudied them and nodded yes with her head as if she had a class of schoolchildren before her repeating their lesson in chorus. Satisfied, she took off her glasses and cleaned them with a corner of her blouse, which was, according to her, the best material in the world for cleaning lenses.

"So, we can go?" Renata asked.

"Damn, it's raining."

"And we'll take the umbrella. Today I brought the big Ferrari umbrella."

"You mean you want to walk?" She stretched her legs under the desk and looked at the workmen in the reserved parking lot covering themselves with newspapers and pieces of cardboard.

"Poor Luì who waits for that naughty Walter. . . ."

"Why, has he gone already?"

"With his usual little friends; they were the first to go. We can take my car, if your legs really don't feel up to it."

"No, let's walk."

Renata was not a good driver, and it was hard to find a parking space in front of the restaurant; Walter was needed, who was always lucky with parking spaces and also good at inventing them when there weren't any.

When they had gone ten meters, they regretted their decision. The umbrella, even if it was big, couldn't protect them from the thin rain, and the cold had not lessened at all. Someone offered them a lift, but Luisa refused.

"We said we'd walk and we will; we're not such helpless creatures."

"I am," Renata protested; she had wound her scarf up to her eyes and pushed her hands deep in her pockets, as close as possible to the warmth of her thighs. "If he picks us up, let's go even with Muto..."

"Muto?" Luisa said shocked. Muto was one of the janitors, a sort of odd job man who busied himself with the most insignificant chores that earned him a bit of extra money. He spoke little and only in dialect. Luisa didn't waste her voice for him; she signaled no with the umbrella and Muto sped off well pleased.

"It's too cold to snow," Renata complained. The restaurant was on the highway, about three hundred meters from the factory. They could already see the cars and trucks coming to a stop at the signal lights, sending up spray from puddles on the parked cars and passersby.

When they reached the light, they crossed with care even though it was green; it was the only one within the radius of a kilometer, and many drivers did not notice it until the last minute. The restaurant was crowded and full of smoke. They expected that. Every day they told themselves they would go early, but they never managed it. They found a place next to the counter of the bar at a tiny table for two. Walter and the rest of the usual group were already having their coffee, and the waiter was taking away their paper tablecloth. Today there was steak or the usual mozzarella. They both chose steak and vegetables, two dishes Luisa did not willingly cook at home. Renata always ate meat at lunch and dinner; the children asked for chops or meatballs, and she pleased them by cooking tons of chops and meatballs, and fried potatoes. Luisa was tired of advising her against such a heavy diet; Renata brought up the examples of her in-laws, big meat-eaters and smokers, who enjoyed excellent health for their age.

"Excuse me, Luì, if I don't take you home," Walter came over to say with a forced laugh, his coat already buttoned.

He indicated a very pretty girl, perhaps a student, who must have been more or less the same age as his daughter.

"It doesn't take much to get you to abandon a lady in the rain." She should have reproached him because his breath smelled of grappa, which the doctor had forbidden him to drink, but she didn't want to spoil his good humor. In fact, he was still eyeing the pretty girl.

"I thought about several, and I chose her," he declared with satisfaction.

"These men," said Renata, who treated Walter like a boy of twenty, handsome and strong, in a position to make any sort of conquest.

Walter left with his office companions, and the steaks arrived, large and well cooked. Together with spicy vegetables, they made a real restaurant dish, and both were pleased. They drank a little wine cut with water; often they left behind half of a small quarter-liter bottle.

They ate quietly without talking. Behind the bar a television set was on, and they felt at home, as if watching the news with dinner. Then they ordered coffee and began to look outside. The rain had slowed and the fog was lifting.

"It would have been better to put all the industries in Sicily," Renata theorized. "Why did they put them here where the weather is always rotten?"

Luisa answered with a forced smile. She had felt strange for several minutes and could not understand why. She greeted other coworkers as they left and lit a cigarette. The student and her girlfriend were also leaving. The door creaked continually. Suddenly, over the young students and her colleagues, over the tables where gnawed steak bones and greasy paper tablecloths were lying, over everything, even the waiters and the bottles on the bar, a cloud descended of ugly smells. Now the whole place was immersed in a disgusting stench of burned fat that turned her stomach. Her heart began to beat strongly; her forehead and face flushed with a stubborn tingling sensation that would not go away even when she rubbed them with her hands. Her lips must surely be white, even if Renata had not noticed; she bit them without effect because they were almost numb. She must try to rouse herself if she didn't want to faint. And to think that Walter had just left! The only one who could have helped her. A bitter liquid threateningly rose to her throat and she pushed it back. Vomit in front of everyone, my God. Spoiled meat, poison, fire in her stomach. My God, she prayed, the muscles of her jaw tightening, my God, help me! Renata continued not to notice a thing; she complained of the smoke and squinted her eyes in annoyance. Damn her, Luisa cried to herself, couldn't she see how squalid that bar-restaurant was? Didn't she smell that unbearable stink of grilled meat? She had to escape from that hellish place right away; she must hurry outside. She threw her fur coat over her shoulders and walked into the open air erect, like a soldier.

It had stopped raining. The air was fresh and smelled of the earth. Her heart continued to beat strongly at the bottom of her throat, and her temples pulsed along with her heart. She had been afraid of not being able to do it, but she had gotten out, and she began to feel better. It was nothing serious. She repeated that to herself, but she began to cry. For an instant she had suspected there was something badly wrong and had been terrified; now she must calm herself. It was a dreadful fear that had not yet left her. The fear of not surviving, in fact. She took long, deep breaths, keeping her eyes closed. The passing cars raised a light wind that did her good.

"You'll see that he'll be faithful to you," Renata said, pretending to be serious. She was wrapped up again, looking out of a thin slit between her scarf and hat. At first Luisa didn't know what she was talking about. Then she remembered Walter's joke and shrugged her shoulders.

"For all it matters to me," she said coldly. But she tried to change her tone. "There was a smell in there . . . to turn your stomach."

"And all that smoke? Bah . . ."

Returning to the factory, Renata started to tell in endless detail about a film she had recently seen. Luisa couldn't follow her but was content not having to talk. She was concentrating on her steps: her legs still trembled from fear and she did not want to fall down. Now and then, Renata stopped to emphasize an important point, and Luisa took advantage of it to rest. She pretended to be interested in the plot of the film, but instead was trying to explain to herself the strange attack. She still sensed about her and in her stomach that smell of burned meat and remembered exactly the sudden misery that for an instant turned everything squalid.

Maybe a shock from the cold, she said to herself, not finding any other explanation. She calmed herself and increased her signs of approval to the story of the film. Despite the cold, Walter had left his friends at the parking lot and was catching up with her on foot. He must have noticed that she was not well, and wanted to give her a hand. It's nothing, she decided to tell him, an old story.

"You must be the first to know that I've decided to leave her," he said, picking up the earlier joke.

"I told you," Renata chimed in.

Walter placed himself on Luisa's left and took her arm.

"Do you remember Scriboni?" he asked with a conspiratorial air.

"That unpleasant queer," Renata commented.

"We were just talking about him in the car. He may have been unpleasant, but he went out like a gentleman. Where's Scriboni? How come there's nothing on his desk? He passed away without saying good-bye to anyone, that's where he is! He's told you all to go to the devil. We made a list of those who died, and we all had the same impression: only the ones who die are good at anything."

"Oh, drop it," Luisa said in annoyance. "If you stopped abusing those poor kidneys, who'd be better off than you?"

"You already have us every day, what more do you want?" Renata backed her up.

"Will you give me a ring when you're finished?" Walter asked, ignoring Renata.

They separated without saying good-bye and went back to their offices. The bathrooms were crowded; employees went in with their kits and brushed their teeth and fixed their hair. Luisa would go later. She didn't want to run the risk of having to see one of the horses from bookkeeping wash her armpits. Her stomach was already upset. But it was precisely one of those girls who was waiting in her office, quietly sitting in front of her desk, and with her favorite shell in her hand. Luisa hastily checked the papers she had brought and gave them back to her coldly.

"It's not your fault, but if they imagine downstairs that we're going to do the work over every month, they're badly mistaken. I'm not going to take stuff like this anymore; you tell them that's just what I said."

As soon as the girl had gone out, her face rather dark, Renata tried to whistle in congratulation of her boss.

"One more time and I'll send her to the little professor," Luisa added, with the tone of someone who will not admit discussion. Then she turned on her screen and went back to her columns of numbers. She needed to be alone for a little while; actually she wasn't looking at the numbers: she made them go up and down for no reason. The insensitivity of her coworkers offended her more and more profoundly. She had been suffering and no one had noticed it, rather they continued to burden her with their problems without looking at her, without giving her the least attention. Fine friends she had, fine colleagues! She remembered the shell left on the edge of the desk, and put it back in the small basin filled with sand from the Adriatic, where there were other, smaller shells all white and shiny as she liked them.

"Shall we put the sea in order, Luì?" whispered Renata. She smiled and smoothed her little beach with her fingers. Her bursts of anger passed quickly; they didn't last more than a minute. It began to rain heavily. Streams of water flowed down the windows, and ever-new drops shone and grew and fell and immediately reformed on the black branches of the tree outside. In the gray sky a flashing radiance appeared, followed by distant thunder. Winter thunder! she thought, rubbing her hands. In the road a car advanced with its lights on and windshield wipers at full speed, its wheels spraying water in high parabolas like fountains. She caught the good scent of rain, and everything seemed beautiful to her, including the green and black bushes that bounded the industrial zone. Beyond, the country began: dark green, black, brown, gray swamps and tongues of fog that glided as in a fairy tale. Her mother had been right: the beauty of nature made one think of God. But then, why was she so upset?

So as not to think about it she resumed her work and spoke for a long time on the telephone with various agents. It began to get dark around four. When she looked, she noticed that Renata had pushed aside her keyboard and was peering outside, her face buried between her fat arms, like a child falling asleep at table. She looked out but could see nothing. The windows only reflected the furniture and fluorescent lights of their little office.

day out of the house ended at six-thirty. She locked the door and got into her pajamas and bathrobe.

This evening she closed her door with particular pleasure, and not only because the cold outside had become intense. Her colleagues hadn't even bothered to look at her during the entire trip. Stupid she for still thinking about it. She was the woman of early morning; she could have their attention only at seven o'clock when they departed for the suburbs, always together to save the cost of gasoline. There was nothing else between them; she could have dressed like Harlequin and no one would have noticed. She could have croaked without changing a comma in their evening schedules.

She quickly made some soup and ate it listlessly while watching the evening news. She didn't feel right yet. She was used to being well and didn't know what to do with herself. Maybe the soup would erase the memory of burned meat that still made her feel nauseated. The usual bad news on television might hold her attention and give her a lift. She covered the canary crouched on its swing and consoled herself with the thought that not everyone had a comfortable place like hers. New curtains made the windows attractive, and the Frau armchair inherited from her mother awaited her hospitably as it did every evening; even the old doll seemed to greet her with its little arm. She stretched her legs out on the footstool and covered herself with the robe. She never had a fixed schedule and fell asleep without the need of rituals. If she liked a film, she stayed awake until it was late; if she didn't like it and there were no interesting programs, she fell asleep out of boredom and got to bed with difficulty.

After a short program of news, a romantic film began. It was a story set in France after the war, and the two protagonists, a man and woman still young, did not have an easy life. When they were finally able to spend a night together in a bleak hotel room, Luisa felt embarrassed and went to get a glass of water. She, too, had had her caresses and her kisses; she, too, had breathed sighs similar to those of the actress, and so she didn't understand why the more realistic love scenes always had this effect on her. She watched for a while but then had to distract herself not to die of embarrassment. Dawn came in the film, and the two lovers separated in the ruins, returning to their humble jobs.

At this point, like a sudden crash against the door or a window broken by a rock, the telephone rang. Luisa let it ring three or four times without answering. She looked at it as if to make certain that it was really hers, but didn't try to pick it up, and it stopped ringing. She almost never made telephone calls and never received more than two or three a week. When Walter and Giancarlo complained of their awful bills, she almost envied them.

She thought that it would have been better to answer; it might have been Walter: maybe there was something wrong with his car and he wanted to ask her to use hers. If that was it, he would call again later, there was nothing to worry about. For now, she hoped that Walter would offer his car for the following week too. During the previous winter, he and Giancarlo had allowed her not to drive until the middle of February, a thoughtfulness that she had so much appreciated that she had given them both a gift of a tie from a famous designer.

She went back to the film just in time to see the hero's former fiancée, who was decidedly more beautiful than the new one. She had a casual manner that might even have seemed too hard, and she spoke with a masculine frankness, but it was understood that she was a trustworthy person, that she had suffered much and no longer believed in men. Luisa decided to be her and curled up happily in her chair.

During the commercials, the telephone rang again, and this time she picked it up promptly. She answered at the second ring, but no one spoke at the other end. She said hello two or three times, then waited listening for a long time. She was able to hear only the distant drone of automobiles. They were calling from a booth. Luisa tried to laugh and said earnestly, "Walter, is that you? Don't be a fool." There was no answer. It couldn't be Walter. A joke without a witticism was not like him. At this point, he would have imitated the voice of the Commendatore or the mayor. Luisa wanted to hang up but didn't and made the mistake of leaving it to whoever had called. Anger made her sweat, and the intense heat that swept through her forced her to unbutton her pajamas and drink some cold water. Then, without a reason, she went to open the small kitchen window and put her head out to look. The avenue was deserted; there was no one in the telephone booth out front; the bar was closed. She didn't suspect anything in particular; she looked down because she didn't know what else to look at. Then, announced by the sound of his steps, an elegant man crossed the street at the distance of the bar. He was walking rapidly, without looking around, conscious of his broad shoulders and the respect they commanded. Luisa thought he must be going to visit a woman. She watched him until he disappeared into a side street and only then became aware that she was getting chilled. Sweating as she was, she risked catching something. Just thinking about it, she felt a thousand shivers. She closed the window and went back to the armchair trembling like a leaf. She covered herself well with the robe and stuck hands and feet under the pillow, but even like that the cold did not go away.

Thinking about it carefully, the attack she had had in the restaurant could have been a presentiment. Until a few years ago she didn't believe in such things as presentiments, but she had changed her mind when her mother died. There had been no signs of worsening on that day, but she had gone into the hospital room with a thought she could not get rid of: that it would be the last time she would see her mother alive. And she was not surprised when, that afternoon, her mother did indeed die. Animals, too, it's known, sense the coming of death. But what kind of presentiment was she getting now? And concerning whom?

She could not think. A sound from outside startled her, and for a few seconds she held her breath. It was only a garage door, a neighbor on his way to bed. Nothing was happening; she must calm herself. She had gotten a stupid, anonymous telephone call, that's all; it happened every day to God knows how many people. They were like the sounds of cars and motorcycles, irritating sounds that come from the city. On an ordinary evening she would have paid no attention to it. All she had to do was warm herself up. Even when she was little it had been hard for her to get warm after she became cold; her mother had had to rub her with a wool scarf heated near the stove.

She tried to follow the film, but nothing about the story of the two lovers mattered to her anymore. She decided to reach out from under the robe and change programs. A political debate would be just right; usually she fell asleep almost instantly. A woman was taking part, a famous politician. She was speaking. Luisa admitted she had a point, and immediately afterward found herself agreeing with another speaker who thought exactly the opposite, and then she shared the doubts of a third because he had a frank way of talking and a man's expression also counts for something. She changed channels but found nothing but conversations and opinions, she who had no opinions and never had any interesting thoughts, who vegetated. She said that often to herself, perhaps without believing it entirely. Her brain must be small, it must lack some fundamental parts, it wasn't normal to understand so little.

The cold did not go away. Wrapped in the bathrobe, she

went to get the thermometer to take her temperature. The column of mercury barely crawled up two or three lines. A sign of tiredness or weakness, as was in fact written on the thermometer. Or perhaps she was getting sick with a bad flu, which would give some sense to all the strangeness of the day. To distract herself, she tried to imagine a hundred faces, her companions in the data-processing course, even two or three friends from school including the one who died on a motorbike, and a teacher, and the tent where she had slept at least twenty years ago on a trip to the mountains, and the old friends of that time, the iron railing in the house where she was born. . . . No, too confusing. It was better to think about Bruno. She expected that she would think about him. She remembered all his curls, which by now must have turned mostly white, but she remembered them as they once were. One small curl twisted around the lobe of his left ear in such a charming way that at first she thought it must be a barber's trick, but it was natural like all the others. She preferred those on his neck, of a soft, pale chestnut like a baby's. The big curls of his head and forehead were also beautiful, almost black, long and vigorous; if you put your fingers into them, you could rest there. While she remembered them she stroked the bathrobe, opening and closing her fingers as if she were petting a cat. Finally the warmth was reestablishing itself throughout her body, and she felt more calm. She remembered an afternoon on the river, she and Bruno seated on a round boulder, the slender floats bobbing on the current in and out of the water like two staggering toy soldiers. The quiet sound of the river which, as soon as she closed her eyes to take the sun on her face, became a live presence flowing in its great rocky vein, and the buzz of a black fly that seemed happy in the sun and free as no man could ever be. Bruno was stripped to the waist with a white towel on his shoulders to keep him from burning and a newspaper folded in four which he never finished reading. There was the smell of the river, perhaps of some distant flowers, and especially the odor of the heated rock, a clean odor that rose together with the heat. What happened afterward? Had they quarreled? Had they talked? She couldn't remember and it didn't matter. She remembered well the curls lightened by summer that stuck out over the edge of the towel. She closed her eyes and could recall Bruno's soft voice. When he spoke he opened his mouth a lot, too much, and made incoherent grimaces, as when, for example, he seemed about to laugh though in fact he was getting angry, or he squeezed her arm with his strong hand and looked as if he would scream, and instead said something tender to her. It was a voice of few sounds, few more than whispered, confidential, suited to his pointless secrets. "You really think so?" Almost all his speeches began that way. And then followed the chaotic explanation that no one understood, but that seemed to contain, judging by his radiant expression, the essence of truth for him, which, just because of its hidden nature, not everyone could grasp. Bruno unmasked the secrets of the world and no one believed him, not even she, although she naturally avoided telling him so. There are those who always talk of politics or of soccer: Bruno was interested in interpretations, and sometimes he was right. Mafia, Freemasons, secret services, police, judges. . . .

She went to return the thermometer to the tiny guest room but kept the robe around her shoulders as a precaution. Heat can be lost in a moment, and it takes an hour to get it back again. And if I can't get it back? If the temperature keeps going down, do you die of cold at a certain point? At twenty degrees? At ten? The light of the guest room, which she used as a storeroom, was only a bare bulb. The bed in the corner, without a pillow, was covered with an old Indian cloth that protected it from dust. As a bed for guests, it had seen little enough service. Underneath it were two old suitcases belonging to Bruno that he had left behind along with a small, rickety desk full of junk. She opened a drawer and found two boxes of medicine, expired years ago, a few handbooks on personnel management and labor law, a yellowed medical booklet, some prescriptions from Doctor Sacchetti. Piled on the desk were four books bought at stalls: a horror novel and three works of strange philosophy, their covers full of spears and magic symbols. She hated them, these books. Bruno had bought them at an awful moment: he couldn't sleep, suffered from strange maladies, or feared that he would suffer from them in the future. Sometimes his breath failed. The doctors said it was nothing serious. But he didn't get better. Months and months almost without speaking. Without even emptying an ashtray, without doing anything at all. She then, with the obtuse desperation of the young, had betrayed him with an insignificant man. There had been no pleasure; it was a stupid tragedy, she thought now, a pathetic incident. If they had had children, he wouldn't have gotten sick, and they would have remained together. They had been fine for a long time, but nothing had been born of them. It was no one's fault. Maybe the poor man thought he was sterile. She had to think of him with affection; Bruno was her youth, which, thank heaven, had been wonderful.

She opened a book at hazard and read two or three sayings of an oriental sage, which struck her as disconcertingly banal. Long strings of words to say the simple things that all mothers say to their children. Bruno had noted something on the margin of the page with his blue office pen, but she couldn't make it out. She hadn't seen him for at least a year, and almost ten had passed since they had separated. Every now and then a formal telephone call to talk of old papers that had been lost. He lived in a new section where she had never been. She knew nothing else; she had lost sight of even the vaguest common acquaintances. She suspected for a moment that he was the author of the anonymous phone calls, but thinking about it calmly, she decided that was impossible.

She closed the door of the room and returned to the television set. They were talking about an African country full of dead people; a row of dry, black corpses was shown at the entrance to a village, watched over by dry, living men who exhibited not the slightest sorrow. An old man sang or perhaps prayed. She knew nothing about this country; during the program they had said its name a couple of times, but she could not remember it. She couldn't even imagine in what part of Africa it was located. They said "Africa," and that was enough for understanding. Sometimes she even mentioned that she was shocked by the African children, but in reality she did not feel any pain, and only that displeased her, to feel nothing. The touched voice of the narrator was also a pretense; it didn't really matter even to him; he was just doing his job.

She began to feel tired, but if she went to bed right away, she wouldn't be able to close her eyes all night. She had to wait for the right moment, she knew that. She had a slight hum in her ears; her head felt empty. Even with an effort, she wasn't able to make herself think only of good things, so the indifference of her coworkers came back to mind, her attack in the restaurant, and especially the cowardly telephone call that still infuriated her. Continually recalling them confused the various episodes of the day into a changeable aggregate in which one thing became the cause of another. After an hour of these chaotic meditations she began to formulate the most bizarre hypotheses, including that of an evil eye, although she had never been superstitious. Her mother had a great fear of the evil eye. A couple of times a year she brought her into the kitchen and subjected her to the test by oil for the evil eye. How much there is! she sighed, and how bad it is! And out came prayers and magic formulas, the interminable singsong of her ancient exorcism.

If her mother believed in it, Luisa asked herself seriously, why shouldn't she believe in it? Perhaps something malignant was really trying to enter her life. Someone hated her, nursed a resentment or a wicked envy, perhaps well camouflaged behind a smile. There are men with envy in their hearts, her mother said, who poison us just by their presence. Who could it be in her case if not Bruno? Her cousin wasn't even smart enough for the evil eye. Looking around a little bit shaken, she noticed the glass eyes of the doll looking directly at her. It was an old doll with a certain value that she kept out in the open in the middle of the new couch. Stretching out her leg, she could touch its silk dress. Its blue-and-white staring eyes looked alive. Many years ago she had seen a film in which the dolls came alive, transforming themselves into killers. She remembered their weapon: a fine stinger hidden in the structure of the arm. They also killed children, which had made a deep impression on her. Not having hearts, they were capable of any atrocity. Suddenly she heard the screech of a truck's brakes from the highway, long and excruciating, which at that hour of night shook her to her nerve ends. To break the tension, Luisa pronounced the doll's name in a loud voice: "Valentina." As if to remind her of their old friendship. But she became instantly aware that it had been a mistake to talk, to make her voice sound in the room. The neighbors, who usually played their televisions too loud and flushed their toilets until three in the morning, seemed all to have gone to bed on this night. After a few minutes, she heard a light tapping on the door of the bathroom. And then she heard the soft sound of what could have been a cloth falling to the floor. A shiver made her flesh creep, and she began to cry. She tried to restrain herself, but a groan escaped from her nose, a whimper that sounded like an animal's cry, and she cried all the more. There's something, she thought, there's something coming into my house. She made an effort to look at her doll again and speak to it in her thoughts; if that little arm moves, if it moves just a centimeter, I'll die. And looking around carefully, she said to the other obscure presences: Stay where you are, I beg you in the name of the Lord, I don't want to see you.

Valentina continued to stare at her, the glass eyes wide open like those of a little madwoman, the arm half raised and the fingers stretched out to grasp a toy that wasn't there. Luisa settled into the armchair; one leg had fallen asleep and she could not restore the circulation. If she had had a daughter, she would have called her Valentina. Valentina. An enormous name. It often happened to her when she was waking up, and sometimes also when she was thinking: a name, or some insignificant details of an object grew gigantic in her mind. If she closed her eyes, the furniture of her room enlarged in size and became visible to her in all their particulars; a little scratch on the desk became a breach where she could lose herself, and the tip of a finger became an irregular extent of scaly skin on an old wound, and her knees rotated like two huge, deserted planets.

My God, she thought, I'm getting the flu for sure. She fell asleep with the fear of influenza, curled up like a cat. Toward four she awoke chilled. The bathrobe had fallen to the floor, and her legs could not straighten out. The doll had no effect on her; the apartment was as usual. If there were a tiny crack between the two worlds, what would prevent her father from passing through after so many years, if only to give her a hug? Her father, who couldn't go for ten minutes without taking her in his arms and covering her with kisses, would not have endured all these years without touching her or showing himself. The same for her mother, because they had been a happy family for the little while it lasted. She managed to get up and limped to her cold bed. She laughed at herself and shook her head benignly. I'm having a second childhood, she said to herself. The real world is the one you see at four o'clock in the morning. Transparent, as if it had just been created, immersed in a peaceful emptiness crossed only by pigeons. She did not have the flu; she did not have presentiments; she had nothing. Everything was going back to normal. She turned off the light and arched her back. The sputtering motor of a passing car cheered her up: they must be out of gas, or maybe the motor was in trouble; in any case, a piece of bad luck in weather like this.

4

THE EFFECTS OF THAT STRANGE NIGHT MADE themselves felt for a long time. Despite her accumulated tiredness, she went to bed later and later, stupefied by hours of television, and every morning she was on the point of deciding not to go to work. She hadn't taken a sick day in years and still had some vacation time to use, but she preferred not to lose the rhythm. For that matter, apart from the irritation of her morning walk to the intersection, going to work did her more good than harm. Walter and Giancarlo, who finally had become aware of her change of mood, did not bother her with questions. Only Renata asked her in a low voice if something was wrong. "I'm tired," she answered without looking up, "I don't know, I feel low." Renata, who had never heard her boss give an answer like that, was profuse with advice, from restorative tonics based on ginseng to the city's miracle-working doctors. Luisa received the advice with a shrug of her shoulders and went back to work, which luckily still managed to distract her. Sometimes she tried to make herself talk of this or that, but as soon as she had decided, the words fled her mind. She asked herself, What did she have to say, after all? To be silent was more restful, and she needed rest.

On the Wednesday morning trip to work, another unpleasant episode took place. They had just left the bypass and were getting into the line at the traffic light, but the narrow road along the canal that they normally took was blocked. They couldn't tell by what at that distance. The driver of the car ahead of them had gone out into the cold rain, and this alarmed Luisa. "Oh my God, it's an accident," she exclaimed, going pale. Years before, she had seen just in front of her the bloody body of a woman fallen with her motorbike, and she had not been able to forget it. This time it only involved a cat just hit by a car. Walter, in order to get off the main road, had pulled up alongside the fatal car, and there they could see the poor animal mortally wounded but still mewing and showing its teeth to whoever tried to approach. It was a very beautiful black cat, young, with thick, shiny fur. The man who had hit it was bending over it, and Luisa hoped he would pick it up or do something to help it. But the man, after having grasped it with a certain disgust by the collar, set it down by the edge of the road and got back in his car. In the meantime, various other cars had formed a line, and someone began to protest. Giancarlo leaned out of the window to see better, and the cat hissed at him furiously. "Poor creature," Giancarlo said, "it's paralyzed." He shook his head with a cold shiver and added, "Go fuck yourself!" No one could tell to whom or what this had been directed. Walter shrugged his shoulders and said, "Better it than a person. . . ."

"Listen to that reasoning," Luisa said indignantly; she had become aware of having stored forever another frightening image in her mind.

"Why," said Walter sardonically, his eyes fixed on the rearview mirror, "would you have preferred a nice old lady?"

"You want to stay on this subject?" Luisa said raising her voice, which came out sounding shrill and with a strong local accent that she didn't like. "Do we have to compare the misfortune of a cat with that of a person? Have we gone mad? If it had been an old lady on the ground, you could have said, 'Lucky it wasn't a boy,' and if it had been a boy, 'Lucky it wasn't a class on an excursion,' and so on. . . . What nonsense are you talking? It's a living creature dying in the middle of the road; if you don't feel sorry for it, it means you don't feel sorry for anything. . . . Poor thing, it was a beautiful cat."

"Seems to me you're taking it too seriously," replied Walter, and the discussion was dropped.

On Thursday morning, after another difficult night full of incomprehensible dreams and sudden wakings, the Commendatore himself summoned her to his office. She went and found him still wrapped in his big overcoat, standing in front of the window overlooking the entrance to the building and its parking lot.

"Aren't you cold over there?" he asked her, pressing his behind against the radiator.

"Yes, they turned on the heat late this morning. . . ."

"I know, I know, but we'll die of cold." Then he rubbed his hands, playing with his wedding ring and a thick, gold ring he must have liked quite a lot, since he turned it with satisfaction around his finger at other times as well. Luisa didn't know what else to tell him and hoped to end this meeting quickly. She expected some instructions having to do with accounting, but she didn't see any papers about. The old man for his part was not in a hurry. He took off his coat very carefully, as if it were fragile, and called a secretary.

"Sit down for a minute, Signora Luisa; we'll have them

make us a good cup of coffee," he said taking his seat in an ample executive's chair where, according to her, he must not be feeling very much at his ease. He looked like a servant sitting in his master's armchair, dressed in magnificent clothing not his own, which he did not know how to wear. The grotesque effect was heightened if the old man lit a cigar, transforming himself into a caricature of the industrialist like those in animated cartoons. Luisa sat down in one of the three armchairs arranged in front of the big desk of pale wood and lit a cigarette.

"I want to ask you for a personal favor," the old man said. "I haven't had time to take care of my private accounts in the last few months, and now I've got a drawer full of overdue papers. The accountants, you know better than I do, are especially good at sending out bills. All in all, I would like it if you could take a look at them. It's extra work, naturally. So, can you take a look?"

"I don't know, I can try," she answered without hesitation, looking straight at him with a boldness that surprised her. She was imagining how he might look from the inside: his old brown veins, the color of cigars; the liver, a darker brown; the brain, gray and yellowish, full of black veins.

"Good, you take a weight off my mind. Look at that, you want to retire, and I'm doing twice as much work. How will I make it without my Signora Luisa?"

The coffees came, and the old man lit his cigar.

They agreed on that afternoon, and she telephoned Walter to tell him not to expect her. She didn't tell him what had come up. Nor did she say anything to Renata, who wanted badly to know and perhaps thought about extracting something during their meal. But at one o'clock Luisa asked her to bring her a sandwich and remained alone in the office, even though she had nothing particular to do. She watched Renata ride off alone in her car and didn't feel at fault. True, she readily admitted, she was putting on airs a bit, playing the boss of the office, but on this day she needed compliments like bread, even if she had to make them herself. Even the Commendatore acknowledged her merits, trusted blindly in her, and wasn't mistaken. She was a person who kept her word; others saw it right away. She thought about the most gratifying incidents of her career, particularly the closing ceremony of the course. She had taken first place, although she was the oldest of the students and had not even tried her hardest. She had also been among the first in her advanced accounting course, from which there had only been five graduates. She should think of that, of her familiarity with the old man for which everyone envied her, and not about the poor cat that died.

But was it really dead? Or had someone braver than she helped it? A broken spine doesn't heal, she thought; nine lives are not enough, not all the lives in the world are enough to prevent a death that must come. She stretched her legs under the table and looked at the sky, heavy with cold rain and snow, that today seemed darker than usual and more threatening. Overhead the clouds were so black they made her think of a well in the sky; the thin, white clouds spiraling upward served only to intensify the terrible depth. Houses and factories looked like toys beneath that sky, and the busy little men became so many ants, certain that their little pile of earth was the center of the world.

Renata came back to the office about two o'clock, complaining of the great cold; she was wearing a heavy mountain sweater over her smock, and she rubbed her hands, invoking the quilt of her bed and the prefabricated fireplace that drew so well. Luisa pretended to be overwhelmed by work. In fact, the office seemed too warm to her; the employees and workers spent a great deal of time complaining, and at bottom the managers were not always wrong. She thought: If the Commendatore were in charge of the city, there wouldn't be those filthy boys in the street, or telephone pranks, or stones and beer bottles thrown against the walls.

Soon after, Renata showed her a problem on the terminal that according to her was insurmountable, but was only the result of her usual carelessness.

"Little girl, take care, these are millions!" Luisa told her. "You have to think about what you're doing, or they'll send you to peel potatoes."

Renata went back to work and from then on did not say a word to her. Now she hated her, Luisa sensed it but did not care; speaking clearly had done her good; she ought to do it more often. The old man paid on time, and they ought to work: that was the rule. The world might be a slaughter-house of cats and men, or a bazaar of stupid toys and stupider young toughs, but at least one rule ought to hold.

In her head columns of numbers and rules appeared in perfect order waiting only to be used. The green figures that ran across the screen had a familiar look like the outlines of a face often seen close up. She worked hard until five-thirty; then the Commendatore called her to say he was free and didn't want to keep her too late. They went together down the red carpet of the main stairway. Muto was waiting for them at the gate; this evening he would drive the owner's big Mercedes. In the Mercedes, even the desolate streets of the periphery seemed more decent, and the sounds of traffic were almost imperceptible. After a short section of the by-pass, they climbed toward a residential neighborhood that Luisa hardly knew. The rain had changed to dense sleet; the streets were deserted, and in the luxurious houses and con-dominiums many windows were lit. Halfway up they made a right turn: it was the via del Giglio, and the gate of the villa opened before the Mercedes' nose.

"Put it in the garage right away, and I'll see you in the

morning," the old man said getting out, "the signora will take a taxi."

He climbed the few steps together with Luisa, muttering about Muto, that he shouldn't have been sent out in a car like that, especially in the snow and ice. The chauffeur had come down with a bad case of bronchitis and didn't get better even though he had sent his personal physician, a professor who taught at the university. A maid opened the door of the house and took their coats.

"This is just the night to keep you late," he said in his most good-natured tone. "I've been lucky, I can't complain, everyone's busy, everyone gives me a hand. . . ." And meanwhile he was leading the way toward the study, which looked stupendous to Luisa. There were many art books, beautiful armchairs, old paintings carefully lighted, and a cherrywood desk, its top covered with leather.

"You know what I'll have them make?" he said, pointing to the big, executive chair. "A good punch with mandarin oranges. Maria, listen," and he left her alone to turn around on the leather chair, hypnotized by a thousand precious objects that for the moment became only hers. The chair oscillated forward and back, and she was being gently lulled when the old man rejoined her with a lit cigar. He guessed her wonder and said, looking around, "Everything you see has a story. It would take a month to tell them all." He pushed a chair next to hers and opened the biggest drawer. "This is the book of the household staff. . . . These are the records of bills and all the expenses. . . ." Luisa had the impression that the old man was hiding his real doubts: maybe he was looking for something in particular and wanted to test her. He hadn't charmed her for many years with that sly manner of his. Before leaving her alone, he said only, "Excuse my wife for not coming to say hello, she knows you won't be offended."

"Of course. Give her my regards, if she remembers me."

When she was alone, she switched on the electronic calculator and began her survey. The private notebooks of the old man were in perfect order and written in a beautiful old-fashioned script. The administrator's and accountant's records, on the other hand, were approximate and barely comprehensible, and various expenses turned out to be undocumented. She also found a bank statement: in this personal account the old man kept parked almost a billion lire in treasury bonds and cash. Strange that he had forgotten it there inside the notebook. While considering this, she noticed a plastic puppet behind the crystal glass where precious statuettes and porcelain were exhibited: an object without value that the old man, many years before, had sold to a cheese factory. In the course of a few months that puppet had found its way into every Italian family, and it had contributed to the building of this very villa, and made her salary, and those of her coworkers, possible. It was a trifle of blue plastic, three or four centimeters high, roughly made with the techniques of the time: it represented a child jumping with joy, holding the point of his funny clown hat with one hand. Before turning back to her work, she thought: If on Judgment Day the Lord asks the old man and his workers, "What have you done in your life?" we'll show him the blue figurine.

It wasn't the moment to daydream. She must concentrate and show herself to advantage. At eight, when she had hardly begun to fill the blank spaces of her notebooks, the old man came in to tell her that he had had dinner prepared for her too, if she didn't mind having dinner with old folks.

"I won't be able to finish this evening," she said, accepting the invitation.

"And you'll come tomorrow morning. Will tomorrow morning be enough?"

"I think so."

"If it's not enough, you can go back to the office whenever you want. Let's stop the numbers now and go and eat. It will be just you and me; my wife has already eaten something, an early dinner."

The dining room was beautiful too, but made less of an impression than the study. In the middle of the table there was a small bouquet of flowers. The maid served a meat broth and poured wine. Luisa felt completely at ease. The old man, who was very polite, had the absent expression of someone with a lot on his mind, and, although he was with her, he continued to be thoughtful as if he were alone.

"What did your father do?" he asked when he had finished his soup.

"He worked for the post office."

"Mine had a store of eight square meters. . . ."

Luisa pretended not to know the story of his father and the little store, of the small trade in coffee that had become a big business, and she listened again to the whole story for the third or fourth time.

They had a grilled fillet with boiled vegetables and finished with a lemon sorbet that the old man could not do without.

"I would like you to keep track of my accounts from now on," he said after looking at her attentively for a long time. "The secret lies in trust. Choose well and have trust. My son should be a magnificent director-general, and instead he's an idiot. They still call him 'little professor,' don't they?"

"Yes, but not to make fun of him."

"Forty-seven years old and they call him 'little professor,'" the old man said bitterly.

Who knows if he was aware they called him "the old man"? Luisa asked herself, restraining a smile. They call him Commendatore only in his presence. But he was "the old man" for everyone, and to see him from close up, under the pitiless light of a low lamp, one could tell that he really was old now and beginning to take on the coloring of death that can't be hidden. A man so old goes on living and thinking, while a young cat with shining fur and two bright green eyes like emeralds lies rotting by the side of a road! Now she understood what had so impressed her: the pride of its mewing against everything, and its elegance, still intact despite the broken spine. A man fallen to the ground becomes coarse or grotesque; easy to imagine the old man with his paunch in the air at the bottom of icy steps, a heavy, overturned animal, unable to get up, with his legs and arms waving in the void. His complaints about his spineless son exhausted, the old man yawned repeatedly and offered to call her a taxi.

"Take one tomorrow morning also, the weather's bad. Come in comfort. And when you're finished, have them call the office and I'll send a car for you. Or take another taxi, if you don't trust that moron."

Luisa had her coat brought and waited together with the old man at the door.

"When it snows, it's beautiful coming back home," said the old man. "If your mind is at peace, you forget everything and enjoy the snow coming down. There's the taxi. Dear Signora Luisa! I've made you work too much today."

He opened the door and the gate for her and, giving her his hand, said, "Be careful not to slip, and thank you from my heart."

He said it often—"thank you from my heart"—his voice becoming a bit artificial, but Luisa was pleased. And she thought it lovely to be riding in a car at that hour under the snow and not having to think about driving. Almost all the lights were out, and even the tire tracks in the snow had a beauty of their own.

On the principal streets there was still a little traffic, but no one was going fast. It was a night made silent by the snow that fell steadily in small flakes. The smell of snow filtered through the windows, and she thought with pride: I'm a woman to whom all the papers are entrusted. Her father and mother would have been proud of her. She knew almost everything about her employer: she already knew the foreign accounts, the embarrassing points of the company's budget, and now she was beginning to find out about the household accounts, the most private matters of a bourgeois family. And she would not have revealed to a single person any of the numbers that had been confided to her.

The driver was listening to the radio and was not keeping an eye on her in the mirror, so she calmly leaned her head on the top of the seat and looked out at the white spots drifting in the darkness. She thought with gratitude of the old man who had paid for the taxi and the refined luxury of snowflakes watched from the warmth of a comfortable seat.

When the taxi left her alone in front of her building, she continued to look at the snow flying slowly around the lamp-posts. She left her coat unbuttoned; she wasn't cold. She thought for a moment of taking a walk around the block but was afraid of being seen by neighbors and quickly opened the door to the entrance. She rang for the elevator and went up to her floor. The landing seemed to be illuminated by a different light from the usual one, weaker and gray, as if the bulb had been changed. She opened her door and closed it behind her immediately, before even turning on the light. As soon as she touched the switch and saw the doll on the couch, she became aware that she had never seen it like that with its glass eyes pointed toward the door. Damn! She had barely arrived home, and already her flesh was crawling. Even the sounds of the canary, who had begun to fly slowly in its cage, had something sinister about them. She covered it and instantly turned on the TV and one after another all the lights in the house. As she hung her coat in the wardrobe, she remembered that she had not yet called Walter. It was eleven-thirty, but he went to bed late. She called him and invented an excuse, not wanting to tell him she had had dinner with the old man, and that she would be returning to the villa in the morning. She told him she was supposed to go somewhere with her niece.

There was nothing good on TV. She stopped to watch a pitchman selling snowblowers, a little fellow who in his obvious dishonesty came through as more sincere than the others. After the snowblowers, someone else offered two beautiful pistols that really fired. "We're at home alone," suggested the pitchman, "we hear a noise in the kitchen. And what do we do? Go to look in our pajamas? And if there were really someone, what would we present him with? Our pajamas? Or maybe . . . with this." He said this with the most serious and trustworthy expression in the world, with his big face of an honest thief. What incredible people roaming the world, Luisa thought, pursing her lips. She shouldn't have drunk two glasses of wine at the Commendatore's. Also she had overdone it with the fillet, and she felt heavy now. She took two Alka-seltzers and went to get ready for the night. She always had to do something else when she brushed her teeth, so with brush in mouth she went back to the pitchman who was reloading his pistol. At that moment the telephone rang.

Luisa bit the brush and did not answer. When the ringing stopped, she began to cry. They really had it in for her; they hated her; they wanted to drive her crazy!

THE NEXT MORNING, at around nine, she called a taxi that took her to via del Giglio. Even though she had slept little and badly, she worked until almost one o'clock, interrupting herself only for the coffee the maid brought her together with some excellent cream pastries. The Commendatore's wife did not put in an appearance this morning either.

Around one a taxi took her speedily to the office, just in time to talk with the old man. She had a list of questions two pages long to show him. She had found something odd involving a blatant error in an entry on the last statement of earnings. The old man gave her the satisfaction of calling his accountant in front of her. "If we don't get along, we can divorce; in business I'm in favor of divorce," he said, rocking in his chair and exhibiting just for her a combative and self-satisfied air. He even winked at her. Luisa was distracted; she examined very attentively the age spots on the man's forehead and face. Death spots, she thought them, drops of death rained down from above.

"Well, how do you like working in my study?" the old man asked after telling off his accountant.

"If I could, I would transfer there," she said to please him. In reality, at the villa she missed her chair, her vista of the access road, even the coffee from the machine. And naturally, her manuals, the collections of fiscal laws. While he went on about the rebuilding of his villa, she continued to contemplate the dark spots. Yes, the Commendatore was a phony and silly old man, at bottom a violent one, but he was also a good fellow, an old man near death who valued her and had never allowed himself a discourteous gesture toward her.

He invited her to lunch, but she understood that he was not serious and said she preferred the short walk to the bar. During the past hour the sun had reappeared, and the snow shone on the roofs of the storage sheds and the bushes alongside the roads.

It seemed wonderful to walk under the sun, and she had to restrain a solitary laugh that would have embarrassed her in front of her colleagues returning from their meal. Even if they never really noticed anything. They didn't even pay attention to the way she walked: the long stride, the straight back, her head high. Almost all the others walked carelessly, the way they dressed. If you stay in the same workplace for a long time, they don't notice you anymore. There was the sun, the snow glittering, and her colleagues hanging about, dragging their shoes like prisoners in a courtyard without a fence.

In that street, among the sheds of the outskirts, in the crowded restaurant on the state highway, they spent their lives. Her father would have found it unbearable. They never discussed things, they worked unwillingly and badly, they didn't read the papers, they didn't understand, they wanted to be slaves! Her coworkers, in their dullness, seemed to respond just like that: we want to be slaves, leave us in peace. And maybe they didn't even notice the sun or preferred to ignore it. They were waiting for winter to continue on its course.

Renata was coming toward her smiling, her coat unbuttoned and hands without gloves. Her round face was the most cheerful among the others, and Luisa wanted to give her a hug.

"How nice we look today," she said, taking her by the arm.

"Thanks, boss," said Renata. "I feel like I'm being reborn today."

"You'll see a frost tonight."

"Tonight, if it pleases God, we'll be in bed. . . . Can I keep you company to the bar? Or do your secret relations with the higher-ups forbid it?"

"What secret relations," Luisa said, "it's only accounts. You sure you want to keep me company?"

"Sure. I want to stock up on sun." They walked a little and she added: "However, there is a secret, I should say."

Her large face was all tenderness at that moment, goodness in its pure state, and Luisa was not able to keep everything to herself.

"There is something, a stupid business. It just makes me angry. I've had three or four anonymous phone calls. They don't say anything, just wait there. . . ."

"Three or four?" Renata said, turning to her and smiling. "That's not so bad, some get hundreds. The usual guys."

"Maybe . . ."

"You know what my news vendor says? He's a very smart man. That the city is always full of crazies. And he sees them all. Poor Luì, you're being picked on by some crazies. You know what you ought to do? Get an answering machine, and you won't give them any satisfaction. The world is full of crazies and shits."

"Well, you and I aren't crazy."

"Except you and me. And a few others."

When they reached the restaurant, Luisa had them put a sandwich and a carton of orange juice in a paper bag for her, and they went back outside.

"On one of my son's tapes there's the story of the Nothing that advances," Renata said suddenly. "It's a good picture. The Nothing is a sort of mysterious enemy that expands. Even now when I talk about some awful happening with my son, I tell him, 'It's the Nothing that advances.'"

And the Commendatore, Luisa thought, is he part of the Nothing or one of us? He's part of the Nothing, she decided, thinking of the plastic trifles. The Nothing always wins. But does the Nothing exist? She didn't know. There was the sun, and there was Renata, good like the sun.

"You know what I'm going to do?" she said, opening her purse. "Lunch from a bag."

They sat down on the cement step around the heating station, and Luisa ate her sandwich hungrily.

"Walter and Giancarlo haven't been around?" she asked, opening her orange juice.

"They've gone to eat by themselves, I think at the pizzeria

in the village. A secret meeting. They're huddling, plotting, even this morning when they arrived."

"It's the first crisis of the Christmas vacation," Luisa said.

"Yes, you're right, it's the crisis. . . ."

5

SHE HATED THEM BECAUSE THEY MADE HER FEEL
the familiar, old hysteria; she hated them especially
for that. As long as it snowed or was freezing the
city remained peaceful enough, but all it took was
one day of sun like that just past and the more im-
patient ones began to make themselves heard again.
In addition, it was Friday evening; she had forgotten that.

For several minutes three or four of the youths at
the bar had been teasing a certain Mauro, and he
answered with a sort of bellow that made her shake
with rage. It may have been just this bellow that
awakened her, and now it would be hard to go back
to sleep. The noises and laughter could keep her up
for hours. They weren't the huge, dangerous young
men of ten or fifteen years ago. Alone, they seemed
like big children made surly by a reproof; they held
their faces down as if they were ashamed of exist-
ing. They were raw, or little more. Stray animals.
Men like her father would have gone down to the

street and chased them away with their mere presence. Her father had thick wrists and strong hands like two vices. His broad nails, always well cared for, made him resemble a noble warrior of earlier times. Not even five of them would have dared to confront him. There couldn't be more than that many right now. Only a vanguard of the army that would be coming.

Spring was on its way. It had never happened to her before to fear it as soon as December. A few days of warmth, and the youths and mosquitoes would be back, the bad smell of insecticides, the television voices, the rumble of motorcycles.

Now they were talking and laughing in front of the garage. Someone had stopped his machine and kept the motor running. They opened and shut the doors continually. There was a little wind, maybe they were cold. Why didn't they go home then?

Luisa thought about turning on the light but decided against it. In five minutes she would have ended up in front of the TV and she would be depressed. It was better to wait for sleep in her bed. The heat was shut down and she felt good under the quilt. The cold air freshened her cheeks. Even if she didn't sleep, she could imagine things. As a girl she could daydream for hours, but now she hardly did it anymore. She did not take advantage of her freedom. She could imagine and tell herself whatever she wanted. For example, did she need a man? She pronounced the word "man" to herself in such a way as made it seem vulgar to her, and she was ashamed. Man was a bright thing, a wretched being with his face always turned to the floor, a glans the color of calf's liver, taut and shining, and sticky stains spewed a great distance. Gobs of very white, warm sperm. Even her coworkers were such things. Even Lorenzo. Who knows what end he had come to. By now they didn't even exchange cards on vacation, but she still became emotional when she thought of him. Elegant, sturdy, strong-willed, capable of overawing even the old man, who in fact did not like him. For three years Lorenzo had been the highest paid consultant in the company; he knew everything about international law, customs regulations, banking systems, the European Community. He had lived in Brussels for five years. Maybe it was there he had learned how to behave so well at table. Because he was also the son of a poor dog, who surely had not cut his meat with such style. He was fifty-three years old, two fewer than she, when they became acquainted. And one day, during a working lunch, he said to her, "Why don't we get married?" He had been married once, to a Belgian woman, but the marriage had not lasted long. Unfortunately, she remembered very little of their conversation. He was less handsome than Bruno, but more charming. Renata called him Clark Gable. He, too, knew the names of all the actors and many more films than Renata. In the evening he changed clothes and went to the movies, even alone. When he was in the city, he lived in the apartment building La Perla. "Why don't we get married?" Perhaps he wasn't really serious. How many sleepless nights that question had cost her! Or rather, what marvelous nights, what dreams, what endless trips to all the cities of the world. He said it in that joking way because he was an intelligent man and knew that a refusal would have spoiled everything. He left her completely free. In the end, the thought of a new married life seemed senseless to her. And above all, exhausting. She had told him, but without it seeming to be an answer, that she was too disappointed a woman; she had let him imagine God knows what sort of disaster with Bruno. Precisely at that time his divorce had become final. While she spoke, Lorenzo listened sympathetically, now and then saying "of course," or nodding his head. He didn't ask her a single question. When he came through the office to say good-bye at the conclusion of his last con-

knees. She mustn't let herself be overcome by panic; she must react. But how? She started to get dressed without thinking about what she was doing, and in a moment found herself completely dressed. Just before, she had been in pajamas in her bed, and now she was ready to go out.

She must get away; she didn't know from what, but she must get away, even if it was still the dead of night and there was a cold outside that she couldn't even imagine. Out, right away, without looking beyond that. She opened the door, ran down the hallway where she grabbed her keys, overcoat, and purse, and threw a quick glance into the living room as she opened the door of the apartment: the doll had fallen, the curtains were blown high, from an open window came wind and darkness. She didn't have the courage to look any longer. She locked the door with her key and waited at a suitable distance for the elevator door to open: luckily the light showed the elevator to be empty. Then, her heart full of apprehension, she descended to the ground floor. Sometimes the young men sat on the steps of the entryway, but she didn't fear them there. She was more afraid of her neighbors in the building, because it was mad to go out so late and in this weather. She didn't even have her watch.

Four or five of the youths were talking in an old car; they were drinking beer from cans and smoking. None of them noticed her as she came out and crossed the street. They didn't hate her, or if they hated her, they didn't know it.

Luisa didn't feel like walking along the avenue; she turned into an alley that led to the old market; it was almost dark but sheltered from the wind. With her hands in her pockets and the overcoat tight around her, she did not feel cold, and her legs seemed happy to free themselves in a rapid pace that warmed her. She was going away and was pleased, escaping from someone who now was unable to get at her, and it no longer mattered who it was. Drunken kids. Thieves. Bruno gone mad. Or something more mysterious that she could not understand.

The streets were quiet, even a child could cross them. At the market intersection, a car of the night police patrol. Several windows were lighted and the small square seemed cheerful, even beautiful: the green cabins with their framework of wrought iron, the old lamps hung at the corners of the streets, the cold, light wind that still smelled of snow. She went round the square twice because she liked it and because she didn't know yet what direction to take. Finally, she chose the street that crossed the center of town and then lost itself in the hills. It had never happened to her to see it deserted. She walked at a good pace but became aware that it wasn't the right one. If you rush, the distances will seem infinite, and you'll be afraid of not making it; great distances are mastered with a methodical gait, not too hurried. She didn't want to return home, even if the fear was going away, and a thousand reasonable explanations were coming to mind: the wind, an open window, a flow of air. She began to worry about her canary. Luckily, the cage was well attached to the wall and shouldn't fall. She was used to thinking only about herself and had forgotten her little animal just at the moment of danger.

A hundred meters farther on a car crossed the street at great speed and made more noticeable the silence around her. Midnight, perhaps one o'clock, and not a passerby in the street. Only Luisa, walking in the direction of the hills. She recalled that she had four or five large banknotes in her purse, and it seemed wise to hide them in her brassiere; but she left one in her change purse because she had heard that robbers get annoyed if they find nothing and become violent. Her cousin, who had been robbed twice, always left a bill in plain sight at the entrance of her place and hid her jewels in a little bag buried in the washing machine detergent.

She ought to have the windows fixed that could be reached from the cornice and change the lock and perhaps also the door of her apartment. She became aware that she was thinking of ways to defend herself as if she were afraid of the whole world, and at the same time she was in the street all alone, very near some of the most disreputable nightspots in the city, and she wasn't in the least frightened. She began to notice the sounds coming from one place that had been closed at various times by the police, but not even that made her afraid, and she did not change her course. Having come abreast of it, she saw three cars full of young men in front of the black doors. She stopped for a moment under a flashing traffic light as if to challenge them, but they did not deign even to glance at her.

She was not afraid. She was only sad and not used to being that way. She began to walk again with less conviction, thinking that she did not know anymore why she was walking alone at that hour of the night. The music's unpleasant vibrations disappeared quickly. One of the cars she had seen in front of the nightspot passed close to her with its radio turned up and drove off in a roar. Only a war could thin them out, these types; hadn't it always been so, in all times? Too many of them. Her father wouldn't have liked to hear her say that, but her father didn't know anything about the stupidity of young men like these. The irritation they provoked, the disgust, not to speak of the disappointment that weighed more heavily than anything else. She imagined the city in arms, people throwing gasoline from the windows or shooting at the youths on motorcycles; she imagined an actual television news report in which they gave a smiling announcement like this: an elderly lady had mowed down with her carbine at least twenty young men, who were passing on their motorcycles under her window. A man had hit the pupil of an eye with his bullet at a hundred meters. The charred bodies of young men and girls who urinated in front of a school. It's our bad habit, said the handsome anchorman with a wink, in the broadcast she was inventing. Young men struck by lightning, impaled on the spikes of fences, torn to pieces by killer dogs.

She had traversed almost the entire avenue with these thoughts, trying to explain them to her father, who as an old socialist rebelled against them and said to her: *This is their way of suffering; at bottom they're not wicked.* She answered him dejectedly: *They disgust me, they disgust me so much.* Until that moment, she wasn't aware of feeling a sensation so specific. To her father she had to admit she was changing. She had always thought of herself as a good woman, but now she was beginning to spoil. It was a law of nature. Everyone learned it. You became more bitter with time, harder. And just as well! This was also something her father never found out, he who never grew old. Maybe the feelings dry up along with the skin. Slowly, slowly, the wrinkles deepen and the spots grow. A natural change; don't blame yourself for it. In place of the feelings, this strange energy had grown up that now enabled her to walk without fear.

She had emerged from the great medieval gate; the center was behind her. The street crossed the wide ring roads swept by the wind and then rose toward the hill. The traffic lights were not working at that hour, and the cars sped along freely in both directions. She crossed hastily and stopped in concern at the beginning of the climb that lost itself in darkness. The old iron lampposts that were supposed to light the way could barely illuminate themselves. The cold had become

she imagined it made slightly golden by the lively fire, with barely a whiff of pepper and the salt crystals not yet completely melted. There was nothing so good in the world.

The muscles of her calves began to hurt and forced her to slow her pace. That stretch of the road became steeper, and for a hundred meters or so it deviated from the old layout of the road; three cement pillars had been sunk in a black garden surrounded by a hedge covered with frost. On the left-hand sidewalk a new railing had been erected, convenient for leaning against and taking in the view. There was also a place to rest your feet, and she put up one for a while and then the other as she looked attentively down at the top half of the central station, which had recently been restored and lit like a church. Not a sound came up from the city; she heard the long soughs of the wind and her heart especially, which was pumping with a strange irregularity and made the inside of her body feel hot, although on the outside her skin was freezing. Like the bushes and trees of winter.

She shouldn't be out at that hour, she said to herself as she stretched her neck muscles for relief. Now that she had given vent to her feelings, she ought to go back; if she went on climbing she wouldn't have the strength to turn around. And she ought to hurry; the cold was becoming unbearable. She decided to go a little bit higher; she wanted to reach at least one cypress. She rounded a curve and found herself facing a crossroad that she remembered well: on the right began the road to the convent, which had years ago been turned into a private school. That was the road of the cypresses. She could see them. She climbed another hundred meters with much effort and chose a tree to lean against. From there the city looked enormous; she couldn't even pick out her own quarter. She rested her neck against the tree trunk and closed her eyes. She imagined never returning home but going on forever, walking for all the time remaining to her and becoming a vagabond, dying of cold on a bench. If it was that she wanted, there was no need to walk so far; she could do it here as well. Her destiny, at bottom, consisted of nothing but disgusting youths under her window and telephone calls without words. She let herself slide to the grass and opened her eyes again. This time she concentrated on the field that stretched away at her feet. It was slightly illuminated by the moon, which made it seem enchanted. Large sections of the grass were covered by frozen snow, white as sheets. She didn't care if her coat was being ruined and her skirt and stockings made dirty by the ground. The wind drove away a great cloud that had been hiding the moon, and the light increased everywhere; on the city three stars also shone, almost identical and at the same height. She closed her eyes and fell into a deep sleep. The wind woke her, and in her half sleep it felt like a woman's hand. She wanted to go on sleeping, but she knew that if she did she would never awaken. She dared herself by closing her lids for an instant, ready, however, to open them again. Now she had decided to get up and go home. The city was beautiful; it was beautiful to look at it with one's back leaning against an old cypress. Why on earth would she have let herself die? What had crossed her mind? Whatever was happening to her came in waves, like sickness, like nausea or fever. Poor Luisa who's growing old, she said to herself getting to her feet. Poor brain that's afraid of everything. Together with the wind, the invisible veil that transforms things had also fallen; now everything appeared banal.

She turned toward home walking slowly, tired and empty. The only parts of her body she could still feel were her aching calves and her feet tortured by her boots. As if in a dream, she crossed back over the deserted roads, then the infinite street that led to the old market. All she could think of was her bed; she cared nothing about thieves or aimless youth. When she found herself back at the door of her

She dozed off and woke up repeatedly until after noon. This had happened to her only two or three times in the last thirty years, and always because of the flu. She put on her comfortable men's pajamas and stood up, enduring the acute pain in her legs. She expected it. She deserved it. Because she was stupid and easily scared. The children in nursery school were playing in the open after so many cold days. They called one another, shrieked, laughed: a swarm of cheerful sounds that drew her to the window. Little men and women followed one another wild with happiness. The hobbyhorses, the ropes, the wooden castle, the swinging tires. They were busier than a squad of workmen. Dear little gnomes, she called them to herself. She ought to learn from them. The little ones are wise and polite; then they quickly grow worse.

She glued a crack that had opened on the doll's face and set it back on the couch with its legs wide apart. An ugly porcelain vase had also broken, and she had ruined a curtain closing the window on it.

A gust of wind had blown in lifting the cloth from the canary's cage. She had been frightened to death by a simple gust of wind. The glass of the little kitchen window had been cracked in one corner, but it held up for the moment. While she waited for the water to boil, she massaged her calves with an ointment that quickly warmed her muscles, and she answered the telephone without fear, ready for a lively response. It was her cousin, who told her that she had called several times since nine o'clock. They were leaving for the country and wanted to invite her to come with them, but it was late now and they couldn't wait any longer for her. "Why don't you come by train tomorrow?" she suggested. "We can have dinner together and then come back in the car." Luisa said that her legs were giving her trouble, but didn't exclude joining them. She turned the coffee off, which had already been boiling for a couple of minutes, and went to drink it in front of the television. The canary hadn't suffered any ill effects from the very long night that had just ended for him too; the sound of the boiling coffee had aroused in him the wish to sing, and he went on at the top of his lungs. "Bravo," Luisa said to him, "what a beautiful song."

Too bad about her legs; she would have liked to go to the country. Until three or four years ago, when her niece, Cristina, was still an adolescent, she had a meal at their farmhouse almost every Sunday. Often after a morning of competition at the gym. Cristina was very good: at thirteen she was one of the best gymnasts in the city and just missed being in the Olympics. A slim body impelled by a flexible and indestructible steel thread. When she jumped like a bird trailing the gymnastic ribbon, or with infinite grace caught the clubs in flight, Luisa's heart of an aunt, even if once removed, filled with pride. Then, at fifteen, and from one day to the next, she had fallen out of love with gymnastics and had become a stupid girl like the others. But, by God, she had been wonderful. And how many great Sundays she had given her. Even the canary, which at that moment was singing as loud as it could, had been a gift from her. Only from Cristina would she have accepted a gift so unsuited to her style of life. From that period the farmhouse was all that remained, and she liked to see it again from time to time. In winter, the restaurant in the village was deserted even on Saturday and Sunday. From her cousin's land one climbed a dirt road sheltered by evergreen shrubs and in an instant reached the ancient gate of the village, which was topped by a pretentious coat of arms: a lion rampant enveloped in two flags. Once that coat of arms had inspired fear in the peasants who came up to the village, and now only a few tourists bothered to glance at it. All fears become ridiculous with the years. Hers, which were already ridiculous at their birth, faded in the passing of a few hours.

She followed distractedly a long television program, yawning and dozing off when she was overcome by it. From time to time she was startled by a noise from the street, but she didn't have enough energy to get angry and excused them all: buses, motorbikes, cars going back and forth. Relatives must have arrived at the apartment below hers, and there were sounds of revelry, but it didn't matter. She wanted to spend the whole day like this, doing nothing, and then go to the country in the morning. She avoided thinking about shopping.

Her legs were hurting less; she would be able to walk quite well tomorrow. Before she went to bed, she made two cooked apples covered with sugar and ate them while watching a talk show about a war she had given up trying to understand, somewhere down in Africa. Then she suddenly came to the decision to put away the doll that was still staring at her. It was a memento of her mother and even had a certain value, but now she only remembered those ugly evenings and thought that maybe it brought bad luck. She took a big paper bag and put it in without looking at it; then she tied the bag with string and put it at the bottom of a wardrobe under a thick layer of old blankets and sheets she never used anymore, almost all of them gifts from her mother The wardrobe was in the small guest room; before turning out the light she looked at it attentively. All her memories were accumulated inside of it. Two or three drawers were filled with family pictures that she hadn't looked at in years. She ought to put up at least one photograph of her father and mother; she had thought about it for some time but never decided. Maybe because she had the absurd feeling of betraying them, exhibiting them in a photograph. It would be like admitting that she no longer remembered their faces. She locked the room and checked the windows and front-door lock. Then she picked out a magazine and carried it to bed under the splendid yellow-and-blue light of the new lamp. She had to sleep again, and for a long time, if she wanted to go to the country tomorrow. The only timely train left exactly at eight. As an exceptional means, so as not to tire her calves, she would take a taxi to the station, which wasn't very far away. She read a couple of letters under the heading "The Editor Responds," and her thoughts drifted off.

She remembered a trip to her grandparents' house in the country with her mother she had made more than forty years ago. The trip had taken an entire day. An old train with beautiful, shiny wooden seats; then a noisy bus full of people. The sun was going down behind the hills, and a wagon pulled by two cows waited to take them for the last stretch. It was a wagon without wheels, a land sled, that left two glistening tracks in the clay road as it moved ahead. She watched now the two tracks, now the big rear hooves of the cows, who made their tails swing and seemed more annoyed than tired. The peasant did not speak, nor did she or her mother. They looked at the blue sky and the hills and the trees and bushes that sometimes brushed the cows and the wagon. After the pungent kiss of her grandfather, who had a beard as hard as the prickles of a dense bush, came the thick steaks, tender and full of sweet blood, smelling of charcoal, and all around were the odors of wine and burning oil. Her grandfather talked, outside the crickets chirped, in the endless fields the fireflies swarmed. The song of the crickets came in waves. The unique sensation of hunger satisfied. How old she was, she said to herself in secret, how many dead ages had passed before her eyes. She had known hunger, had been pulled by cows, had seen houses without electric lights, and heard the silence that must always be there, at least at night. Crickets, owls, and now the youths with their car radios!

Why were they talking so loud; there were only four of them! They had already been disturbing her for a while and she pretended not to hear them. They talked loud because they liked to disturb and for the same reason they played their music loud: they did it on purpose. On the floor below they were playing cards, and every now and then they laughed and shouted all together, women and men. They were drunk, possessed by wine and cards, and even their laughter was frightening. This is hell, she thought with deepening sadness. Hell really exists. On the other hand, there's no trace of paradise. Perhaps it swallows up the blessed and carries them safely far away. Her mother was a believer; her father put his hopes in the new man. Later, he stopped believing that the new man would ever exist, and her mother, too, began to doubt and said on her deathbed: "To bring children into the world is irresponsible. Afterward, who helps them? Maybe your father was right; in fact, the poor man has never been seen again, not even in a dream. . . ."

Was her father right? He who had read the pamphlets that spoke of monkeys and man, and who said that God is man himself, that God is made in the image and semblance of man, and in fact it is written Son of Man, and who always added that there had been deliberate falsifications, and who seemed to see before his very eyes those betrayers of poor folk. "It's like at the fairs. There are the cheats' helpers who say they won and show the money, and the witness who pops out too, and the one who persuades himself and begins to play so as to pull the chickens in after him."

She who wouldn't lie on her income tax for even a hundred lire because she felt herself being observed! The saints, however, in their caves of sand, the saints who wrote kneeling on stones with a light shining over their heads, were they

out together; then in the space of a couple of hours she couldn't stand her anymore and for several weeks, as long as the memory of her disappointment lasted, she didn't call her or invented excuses if she was called.

She thought the train was comfortable and full of interesting people. Sitting near her was an odd-looking, elegant little man. At first, he looked to her like a girl dressed up like a man, then a boy on a day off from private school, and when she got a chance to look at him well, she found him attractive. He was not a boy but a man of uncertain age, roughly between thirty and forty. He was almost a dwarf but well proportioned. He had black hair combed back, a wool blazer, a handsome coat folded over next to his suitcase; but what especially struck her was his tie, knotted under the open collar of his shirt, of a dark blue like the socks that could be glimpsed under his corduroy pants. He was at ease in all ways: in his unfashionable dress as in his manner of presenting his ticket, which in his well-manicured hands looked like a ticket for the Trans Europa Express instead of one for the second class in a modest *diretto* that stopped at every station. When he put a cigarette to his lips, she hurriedly took out one of hers, and he, always with great elegance, leaned forward and held out his silver lighter at just the right distance. They exchanged a smile without speaking. Luisa did not have the courage to disturb him with an effort at conversation. She would have liked to hear the voice at least of so strange a man; she imagined it light, like that of a well-bred young person. She thought she would have liked to talk with him and become his friend, because he certainly was a good and sociable person. He was so serene: that in particular struck her, with a serenity ripened by sufferings the nature of which she could not guess. When the train reached the city, she hoped that they would say good-bye, but it didn't happen. It would have happened in one of the old compartments, but unfortunately not in an open car like theirs, big as a street full of unknown people. In the taxi she continued to think about the little man; she didn't want to forget him right away. They could have become friends. She would have spoken of the disagreeable sensation she had coming home, as if it no longer were hers, and he would have understood. She would gladly have prepared Sunday dinner for him and would have gone to the movies or the theater with him, or simply for a walk in the public gardens. There might have been something even more between them; that wasn't to be excluded. He was not at all ugly, on the contrary, he emanated a very distinctive charm and must be delicate with women. She would have liked him beside her at that moment; she would have liked to be caressed. It could still happen to her, why not? If she frequented other circles she might feel less arid. For years she hadn't met anyone she could consider interesting, and the life she led offered her fewer and fewer opportunities. For this reason too, she had little desire to return home.

It was cold; the taxi driver complained about the short distance of her ride. She excused herself as she got out of the cab, saying that her legs hurt; they really had become more painful. It had been a mistake to walk from the farmhouse to the village; she had asked too much from her tired legs. In front of the bar there were only two cars with their windows misted over, full of young men who paid no attention to her. She went up to her floor and put her key into the lock, which opened at the first turn. Usually she double-locked it, but she must have forgotten to do that in her haste to leave. She took off her coat and went into the kitchen to heat some milk. Apart from the pain in her calves, it had been a good day. The youths in the street were tearing up a cardboard box, perhaps from a pizza, but they were not talking loud and kept the radio turned off.

While she fixed the milk, which seemed unresponsive to the flame, she recalled the door of the house. She was sure she had locked it completely, as she always did, even when she went out to shop. She must have forgotten. For several days she had left everything open, windows and doors, and now she was frightened. There now, she had barely thought of being afraid, and already it seemed to her that she heard a sound. Was there someone in the house? No, it was just the sound of the refrigerator. She lowered the flame and went to turn on the lights in her bedroom and bathroom. No one was there, not even under the bed. She was on her way back to the kitchen when the telephone rang. It was two steps away so she picked it up before it rang a second time. She didn't hear the usual street sounds, only a humming that gradually turned into a whistle. She put down the telephone and ran to turn off the milk, which was boiling up in the pot. She added a little cold milk and filled the cup. If she had the telephone number of that little man, she would have been able to describe her fear to him at the same time she was feeling it. Who knows how many times they had called while she was away. She tried to divert herself by imagining the sea that always relaxed her. The old pension where she went with her mother: lunch at one o'clock, dinner at eight, pasta with real clams, a slice of she-didn't-know-what-kind-of fish, and the low wall next to the sidewalk, with weeds beyond it and then the beach, the sea calm as a pond.

She had just put on her pajamas when the bell rang, so softly that she wouldn't have heard if it hadn't rung twice more in rapid succession. She knew that something was going to happen, she sensed it. Although shivers were making her skin ice cold, she picked up the intercom phone and said hello. She expected a terrible silence, instead she heard coughing. And then she heard a voice mumbling excuses. It was Bruno.

"You could at least telephone," she said.

"Two booths broken, I swear, I was cut off twice. I could use some photographs, if you still have them. But if you want, I'll come back some other time."

Luisa opened without saying anything else. So Bruno had decided to show himself openly. He must have come in during the afternoon, and going out he forgot to double-lock the door; it certainly had also been him the other night. He wanted to scare her to death. He wanted to hurt her. She thought of calling the police right away, and instead opened the door and went to sit down in an armchair. She turned on the television, too, so as to make a certain impression. Just as the elevator door was opening, she decided to turn the light down a little, and received him in half darkness, her eyes fixed on the television which she did not see at all.

Bruno did not approach. He stopped before his old room.

"It'll only take a minute," he said and went into the room. She only saw him for a moment: white hair, many more wrinkles, the same frantic look under two bushes grown out of all proportion.

He made her afraid and enormously curious. She would have liked to check on what he was up to; she heard one drawer after another being pulled, and it was not his room anymore, she shouldn't allow him to search it. But she said nothing. Bruno, she could tell by the sound, had sat down on the bed and was rummaging through the photographs. Because of his chronic sinusitis, he breathed noisily, a sort of prolonged F emitted when he inhaled and exhaled, with two different tones. He breathed and maybe thought of harming her. But why?

"The one with the pike, you remember it?" he asked her at one point.

"I don't know where it is," she answered, "I saw it many times, but I don't know where it is."

He took up his rummaging again and went on for a long time.

"I found it," he announced at last. He came out of the room but did not move much closer. He was turning the old black-and-white photograph in his hands. He giggled and said, "It's better if we don't look at one another. . . ."

"Very kind of you. That can be arranged as you wish," she said, turning the light down a little more. "Would you like a grappa?" She went to pour him the drink and did not pause a second more than necessary in front of him. His face looked thinner and his abdomen a little swollen, sickly, but especially she found him unfamiliar. Nothing remained between them, not the slightest attraction.

"I spoke for myself, you understand," he mumbled, as if he had been late in catching Luisa's irony. "I said it for myself."

Then he calmly drank the grappa, savoring it noisily and with broad facial expressions, perhaps in order not to have to talk.

"Are you all right?" Luisa asked.

"Yes . . . well enough . . . I was never outstanding for my health, but all in all . . ."

"And you don't have anything else to tell me?"

"No, nothing new. . . . I wanted to come by for three months, but one thing and another. . . . I fish, go to the country. . . . Giovanni's dead, did you hear? The one with the Lancia."

"Poor man. What of?"

"A stroke and he was gone, a month ago. He went out of a bar and fell on the ground. That's the only news, it's something, eh?" He looked at his pike and changed the subject.

"It's a bet, this shitty fish . . . they don't believe I caught it. . . . I remembered there was this picture . . . beh, I caught it."

"Yes, you caught it."

Bruno drank another swallow and held the picture at a distance, as old people do.

"What a day, eh? And we were going away. . . . It always happens like that. Are you all right?" he asked with an embarrassed grimace.

"A little tired." She looked at him carefully and added, "I've been getting strange telephone calls. It rings and they don't say anything."

Bruno was undisturbed; he didn't react at all as far as she could tell.

"They're repairing the main exchange. Working on yours too. Or maybe it's an admirer, who knows?" He laughed through his nose but then turned serious. "You were going to bed?"

"It's a little late."

"Of course, excuse my bothering you, excuse me." He finished off the rest of the grappa and moved toward the door. He still had something on his mind because he stopped and looked at her shaking the photo.

"Seriously, I've been talking about myself. You haven't gotten older at all; you're still the same."

She tried to smile but was unable to answer at all. She was certain now that he was not the caller, and in a few seconds she repeated it to herself a thousand times. Bruno only wanted a photograph. She closed her eyes for a moment, and when she reopened them, he was next to her. Bruno's chest and arms were in shadow, while she was under the light and felt ill at ease. Bruno's hand approached her face and gently touched her cheek. He didn't dare caress it; he limited himself to touching it. Then he pushed the hair behind her ear, as he had done thousands of times. Luisa could not speak or move. She only felt the weight of her hair behind her ear. She remained still even when he kissed her on the mouth. A light kiss that made her shiver.

"Excuse me," Bruno said. She shook her head no, to tell him it didn't matter, and not even then could she speak. Bruno turned toward the door and said good-bye with one of his forced smiles. "All the best," he said before going out. Luisa closed her eyes and listened to the sound of the elevator going down. All he needed was his pike, and he hadn't had a thought of injuring her. Now he was getting out of the elevator, and in a moment he would open the door; there, now he had gone away, perhaps forever. For a few seconds the sharp scent of the grappa he had drunk remained. Her stupid premonitions! She had blamed him unjustly, and now she was ashamed. She had also been rude, while he, in his way, had been as courteous as possible. Excuse me, excuse me; he had asked to be excused more times than she could remember. He wanted the photo of the pike. And she still recalled his mouth; she felt regret for it. Poor, gentle, beaten dog. With his inflated paunch and sunken cheeks, and his eyes deeply set, almost hidden by wrinkles. Who knows what he eats and drinks. And that old shirt that no one had ironed for him. She didn't close her eyes all night. She had been unkind and unjust. As when she had sent him away ten years before. She didn't like anyone anymore, she said to herself dejectedly; she was an old, unsociable goat.

She didn't turn on the light that night; she had too many thoughts and she remembered better in the dark. For example, Bruno as a young man. His sturdy chest, the hair around his almost black nipples, his sex big and dark, soft as a cloth. How handsome he was, even too much so for her; she could see that clearly in the eyes of her coworkers. Renata had never even come close to a man like that. The curls around his ears. How many hours she had spent looking at him.

Dozens, hundreds. Now they came down to a few confused minutes. What a waste, what a ruin of time. When she recalled the exact words she had spoken to him so many years before, she began to toss and turn in the bed. "You're an unbearable neurotic!" she had shouted at him. "You're a worm!"

To be sure, he had done nothing to stay.

But he had his pride, and she had wounded it.

They had not become a family; they had broken up over an undeniable failure: failure as a family. No children. She would have been better off staying with him, she admitted with the first light of dawn. Love or no love, they would have helped each other. He wanted his pike, poor dear; he had really fished, and she could really testify to it. And if, in fact, the pike had only been an excuse? If he had needed to talk to her? Tension had brought on a distinct stomach acidity, and she had to get up to take a couple of pills.

She continued thinking about Bruno in the office, too, without feeling the tiredness of her sleepless night. The only acceptable solution seemed to her this: Bruno was having a hard time. He was not well and had no one to help him, also because his character was such that he could not ask others for help. He didn't even talk to his best friends. Yes, that was the only explanation. The photograph of the pike was an excuse. He had asked her for help and she had not understood. Now that she knew, she must do something. If he wasn't well, she would help him. Even if she was not in love with anyone, something good still remained inside her.

She looked for Bruno's telephone number and called two or three times without finding anyone. Better like that. Certain things one didn't talk about on the telephone. They should be spoken of in person. She made a photocopy of the street map and worked out the best route to his house, then folded the sheet and stuck it in her purse.

She said nothing to her workmates. As soon as she

reached her house, instead of going up she went directly to the garage. She hadn't used her car for weeks; it had been years, in fact, since she had taken it out in the afternoon, but this evening she was not afraid of the traffic.

Once past the park, she saw that the traffic was running smoothly; the principal flow was from the suburbs toward the center. She crossed the great railroad bridge, and after a few kilometers, with the copy of the map on her knees, she found herself in one of the new neighborhoods of that district. It was not ugly; there was a bit of green, and each group of houses had its own parking spaces. The lampposts for the streetlights were even quite graceful with their rounded forms and the soft, yellowish light they shed around them. Finally she found the number she was looking for and parked right in front. That was where Bruno lived. Every day for years he had returned home and opened that door, picking out the key in the yellowish light of the street lamp. In the flowerbeds that adorned the entrance were two large pittosporum bushes that had survived the frost. She pressed Bruno's bell and moved closer to the intercom. She cleared her throat in order to say her name distinctly and perhaps with a hint of irony, but no one asked her for it. She rang again, longer, and waited, looking through the glass of the doorway at the lights of the elevator and the entranceway of the house. There was a large houseplant next to the elevator, thick leaved and a little faded, with big leaves shaped like a hand. Something living that Bruno saw every day and that he certainly contemplated as he waited for the elevator. Then the elevator rose to the third floor and returned to the ground floor. A boy with an overcoat too long for him came toward her and looked at her in an unfriendly manner. In order to avoid his stare, she turned then to examine Bruno's bell and noticed that under his name there was another surname written on an adhesive strip. The boy was far away by then, but the door, pulled by an automatic arm, had not completely closed, so that without having actually decided, she found herself in the lobby in front of the mailboxes. There the names were spelled out in full. Next to the unknown surname was written: Daniela.

Luisa blushed and hurried to the door, which however had closed. It took her several seconds to find the push button to open it, and she finally ran from the building like a thief. If she had met Bruno, she would have died of shame. She had been moved to pity, poor fool that she was, while he had been living with someone else for who knows how long. This time he had been right, she was the idiot. She started the engine and pulled away without releasing the brake, stepping on the accelerator as if she had never done it before. When she reached the main road, she slowed down and drew a breath. Now she could even laugh at herself and tell herself, "Poor Luì, poor Luì," with her spine relaxed against her seat and her head leaned back slightly against the padded headrest. She really didn't envy her, that Daniela, not at all, let God be her witness, and she did not miss Bruno in the least. Hadn't she been at peace for years, without interruption, ever since the day of his departure? What a fool she had been about to make of herself. She imagined herself in Bruno's dining room, before a coffee made by that Daniela, and his eyes staring at her, and the embarrassment that would have overcome her in those terrible few minutes. She had escaped from an enormous danger and had been very lucky.

The relief following her dangerous escape lasted only a short while. Her chest again filled with anxiety, and she felt alone as if she were at home and not in her car a few meters from hundreds of other drivers. She had been stupid not to think of that before: she mustn't be concerned about Bruno, but about herself. She was behaving very strangely, going out at night, making unforgivable mistakes like leaving a window open and forgetting to lock her door. Sooner or later, if this kept up, she would go out in her pajamas and begin to talk to herself.

A little before the railway bridge, the traffic began to thicken, and it took ten minutes just to cross the bridge. As she was turning toward the center, she noticed that she was bathed in perspiration. She opened the window and at the first red light slipped out of her coat. She was hot in December, and at eight o'clock in the evening! How could all those women she saw in furs bear it? She found her street full of cars, with real jams in front of the restaurants and movie house, and naturally around her house, where a car blocked the entrance to the garage. She wanted to blow the horn but limited herself to flashing her lights furiously, and after a while a young man came out of the crowded bar and, chewing on something, calmly moved his automobile without excusing himself and not in the least intimidated by the look of reproach which she fixed upon him. If she had been a man, she would have gotten out and smacked him. She locked the car in the garage and went up to her place in a mood that was more and more bleak. She kicked off her shoes in the hall and went to stretch out on the couch. It was too hot. She pulled off her dress and went to put on her pajamas. Then she remembered that she had not given a thought to dinner. There were some roulades with vegetables in the freezer, but she was not hungry. Better skip dinner and go to bed right away. She felt dazed, confused. The heat of winter! The traffic that droned like a huge animal! Thus had her stupid generosity been rewarded.

7

WINTER DID NOT LAST LONG THAT YEAR. AT EAS-
ter it was as warm as summer, and people were
dressed lightly. Luisa had resumed driving one week
out of three in turn with Giancarlo and Walter,
who had made her the gift of another winter without the torture of having to drive. By now it was
stronger than she; if there was fog or it was snow-
ing, she did not feel she was able to take the wheel.
She felt a cold sweat just thinking about it. From
January on she went regularly twice a month to the
via del Giglio, usually on Saturday afternoons. She
worked for two or three hours at the desk with the
leather top; then she had tea and went home by
bus. It was an easy job for an accountant at her
level, and she was paid, according to her, even too
generously. The Commendatore was more at ease
now that he had entrusted his private accounts to
her and missed no opportunity to show his gratitude. With her first extra check Luisa bought herself a beautiful dress that she had not yet worn. She

took it out of the wardrobe almost every day and tried it on in front of the mirror. In order not to wrinkle it, she held it against her chest with the tips of her index fingers.

She continued to receive some anonymous telephone calls, but she no longer paid attention to them. The central exchange was, in fact, being replaced, and in a few months even the numbers would be different. Her new number contained three sevens, and for this reason she liked it more than the preceding one. She immediately memorized it, verifying with satisfaction that she remembered all her old numbers, including those at work. Her memory was still excellent, and in general her health could be considered reasonably good. Eating very little meat and a lot of vegetables did her good; she must have been poisoning herself for years eating at that damned restaurant. Every now and then, she felt a touch of fever, the sign of a stubborn weakness and an unmistakable loss of tone. The arrival of hot weather had never been a good time for her organism.

In spring, more serious problems imposed themselves, not to be resolved by diet. She can get used to a telephone ringing now and then; she cannot get used to a disturbance that is never the same and becomes worse and different every day. She can even get used to passing trains but not to the unpredictable and variable noises of the youths, who could be quiet for a night or two, immersed in their dull hubbub, but then suddenly exploded, and there was no way to calm them down for days on end. She was witnessing a new generational change, she told herself in alarm. She had never heard them yell so loud and for so long. They were always there, afternoon and evening; they never had anything else to do. The warmer the days became, the more the army of idlers swelled; the number of motorcycles increased, and the motorbikes, and the enormous mountain jeeps.

During the Easter vacation, in order to distract herself a little, she decided to give herself the gift of a short trip outside the city. She put on the new dress and took her car out of the garage before the young men arrived.

There was a good deal of black in the new dress, but it would have been called yellow by whoever saw it. Great lemon-colored petals on a background of gleaming black. It looked very good on her, especially in daylight, which brought out the warm tone of the yellow. She tried not to notice, but in a corner at the bottom of the steps were two puddles of red vomit left by the usual nighttime pigs. In rage, she stepped too hard on the accelerator and made the tires screech on the cement. They had robbed her of pleasure in a new dress; they dirtied everything. She hurled her ritual curses and began the trip at a moderate speed. There was no traffic; the trees along the avenues and in gardens were putting out new leaves; the sun was beginning to reach the highest branches. It was a splendid morning. The sky was bright blue and the houses were still in shadow, so that the roofs were silhouetted darkly against the blue and gave a sweet sensation of peace. In the pond of the park, half dark brown and half shining blue, swans and mallards sailed along with extraordinary elegance. Beyond the park, she took a narrow road that climbed the hill. She had a new dress; it was absurd to keep it locked up in the wardrobe, and she could allow herself a good meal out every once in a while. She always ate the same things, so naturally her digestion was poor and she had no appetite.

In front of the villas and on the balconies, flowers of every size were displayed, most often red in color. Daisies, hibiscus, hyacinth, geraniums, and many others that she did not know. On the hill, silence and cleanliness reigned. The great advantages always belonged to the rich. Young men with their machines from up here, no doubt, were unable to find places big enough to gather in, so the children of the rich went down into the city at night to plague the neighborhoods.

A few years ago, Walter had taken her to dinner at a fine restaurant with a terrace that must be in this direction. She didn't remember its name and hadn't been able to make a reservation. She passed easily through the suburban districts and finally left houses behind. She had always liked the bare hills scored with furrows. Buildings were few and for the most part abandoned. She pushed on for many kilometers without meeting anyone. The restaurant with a terrace was not to be seen. The winding road began to tire her, the thought of the way back was spoiling her pleasure in the trip. Finally, from the top of a hill she recognized the group of houses that announced the presence of the restaurant. She was so tense that during the last few kilometers she had driven in the same gear and the engine complained.

The restaurant's parking lot was shaded. There were only three cars, two of them with foreign license plates. Too early for the usual clients. The tables on the terrace were already set, and a light breeze stirred the white tablecloths. In the middle of each table was a beautiful pink carnation, and she felt the need to smell hers, which, however, did not give off the intense perfume it seemed to promise. She decided to eat fish, even if it was more expensive. Who could stop her? This is freedom, she said to herself. From the terrace she took in the splendid vista of furrowed land and the huge white sky full of mist. The clay of the furrows was drying in the sun. The tagliolini with cuttlefish ink came to the table, and she thought they were excellent. Then she had stuffed cuttlefish and unhappily had to leave more than half on her plate. The waiter was concerned to ask if there was something wrong with them, but she praised them lavishly and almost begged pardon for herself; unfortunately she was not hungry anymore. She had drunk only one glass of wine, but she was beginning to sweat. She wiped her forehead with a paper napkin, hoping that the waiter and foreigners would not notice that a fire had been ignited inside her. It had not happened to her for a long time, and it made her angry. Her trip was ruined. Heat waves came up from the furrows distorting the outlines of the distant green hills where the city began. The Germans, who had chosen a sunny table close to the railing, were also admiring the vista and talking softly among themselves. They were a family. The parents were more or less fifty; the children, a boy and a beautiful girl, were in their twenties and behaved like adults, smiling without sarcasm and rarely intervening in the conversation. Northern people, restrained in their movements. A different race, without vulgarity, respectful of others and of public places.

She wanted to make a good impression on them, and even if she felt ill at ease, she tried to control herself, concentrating on the currents of heat rising from the furrows or following the erratic path of flies under the white cloth that covered the terrace. The waiter brought her coffee and again she felt flooded by fresh perspiration.

"Could you bring me a digestive with a lot of ice?" she asked him. She did not have a preferred brand; she never drank them; and she let the waiter choose one. The coffee and liqueur made her sweat all the more. By now it was useless to try to dry herself. The new dress stuck to the skin of her legs and back. Two streams of sweat descended from her neck and her chest. She lit a Multifilter and closed her eyes. She wanted to cool herself by sucking an ice cube that still tasted of liqueur. She must keep still and hope for a breeze. Every now and then a breath of wind rose along her legs, but it disappeared immediately like a wave in the sea, and she began to hope for the next one while dreaming. Her father seated at the window, very warm in an undershirt unfortunately not immaculate. The feminine odor of her mother in summer sometimes when she fanned herself with a broken fan.

Two large drops of sweat ran along one cheek and fell on her dress. The young German said something funny and the others laughed, momentarily going beyond the threshold of audibility. Sincere, intimate laughter. Then the wind came back, and this time it lasted. As cool as a baby's lips. The sweat dried and quickly reformed, but less copiously. Perhaps the temperature was falling.

In the last twenty minutes she had only moved her right arm. Her body did not respond to her. The dregs of the liqueur in the glass and the two yellowish cigarette filters nauseated her. The waiter was serving a second ice cream to the young Germans, and she asked him for the check with a nod. She touched her forehead and was comforted feeling it dry. Her dress, too, was drying. A thin cloud had appeared on the far off hills, and she imagined it as a gigantic pedestal where a young Jesus could materialize who, from that great distance, grandiose as he was, looked directly at her at that table and sent her his paternal forgiveness. It's precisely you, Luì, precisely you I want to see. Even a hair of the lowliest of the low is of great importance to me. I love you too. I am the loving master of the lonely, and the heat you feel is my flame, and you must never complain of it. Then she imagined the Mother of Jesus, who covered the whole sky in a mysterious flight of blue, while the furrows smelled of roses and of Her, and the whole world became a paltry ball of earth that she took in her fingers, and the whole sky was filled with her gaze, and her gaze was fixed upon Luisa, blue and gentle. Luisa felt obliged to make an answer, so she recited the Ave Maria from beginning to end.

When these religious fantasies vanished, she called herself a hypocrite. First she filled her belly to bursting, then she said her little prayers. As if she didn't know that there was nothing more unheard than prayers. The sky was full of beautiful prayers. She ought to keep her feet on the ground and take account of the odor of cuttlefish, the bitter taste of the liqueur diluted in the ice, the itch of drying sweat. She went home with the sad conviction that her strict diet would never be changed. She could no longer eat as she once did; she must resign herself.

AT THE END OF THE SHORT EASTER VACATION, she was glad to return to work. At five minutes to eight on a Tuesday morning, she opened her newspaper on the table and drew a sigh of relief. Renata, on the other hand, had no wish to be in the office and shook her hair over the keyboard reciting mournfully, "It's beginning again, *oy, oy,* it's beginning again," and before that Walter and Giancarlo had complained of the same thing and had chanted an advertising jingle like two madmen. Luisa decided to ignore Renata and her other coworkers as they went by grumbling with their paper cups full of coffee or chocolate and buried herself in the abundant news of the day, which offered her a story of exceptional interest. She looked again and again at the faint picture of a frail and mustached old man and announced to herself, Here is the man. She absolutely must remember to take the page home. Here is the rebellious victim, here is the hero! They had tormented him for twenty years. Generations of young monsters. And there was one of them, in a photograph justly smaller, in his capacity of the "slain." The journalist could not allow himself to sympathize with the pensioner, but he laid out in detail his long and impeccable life of toil and the sincere praise of neighbors who called him polite and reserved. The person who lived opposite him said, "In thirty years I never heard him raise his voice." The youth displayed the thick neck of the dull-witted male. And two stupid pop eyes. Unquestionably one of those who laughed loudly and went *Uuuuh! Ooooh!* . . . An animal. God knows how many times he had been outside the bar and had urinated on the shutter of her garage. In his favor the reporter had noted only "the indescribable grief of his family." Act 1: The old man yells something at the youths who are making a racket in the courtyard at one in the morning. They tell him to go to hell. The same thing happens with the police to whom the man has recourse for the hundredth time. The uproar grows. The old man throws some water on the lot of them. The youths start to throw stones and break a pane of his window. Act 2: The old man, God help him, fires a shot at the biggest of them and hits him in the head. He dies at dawn in the intensive care unit. The old man is taken to jail. His face is serene. He's a good man! Here's someone tormented by noise and filth, abandoned by everyone, and finally purified by revenge, which still emerges among honest men. Maybe he was crazed, says the journalist, but deep inside him the journalist has also intuited the truth, namely, that the old man had finally come to his senses, that he had recovered his pride in being a man and a citizen, and that he was no longer a trembling worm shut up every night in his hole.

"Take a look," Renata said, "the little professor is early this morning, and he's alone."

Luisa looked at the main gate; the little professor made no impression on her.

"The old man must have left for the baths," she said drily.

"Poor little professor," Renata said mockingly, in her little girl's voice.

"Poor you, if the old man dies," Luisa said, returning to her reading although the head of personnel was making his rounds.

An old pensioner against the whole world. His old double-barreled shotgun against the young monsters. She thought of writing to him, of going to his trial and giving testimony before the judge. Your Honor, I too am a victim like this poor man you have imprisoned and who now presents himself for your judgment. Every human being has a right to silence, at least at night and at least in his bedroom. At your house on the hill, Your Honor, where you no doubt live in a small neighborhood of judges, you don't know of these things, but in the center and in so many other districts one can't survive anymore. The smell of piss, Your Honor, the smell of a latrine right in front of the sisters' school, and pieces of bottles, and cans, and worst of all the damned motorcycles of all sizes, may God damn to hell whoever invented them and sells them! *Ruuum! Ruuum!* and then the laughing and the yelling at two in the morning and even three. Your Honor, you are about to commit a grave injustice with respect to this man; he's being treated like a criminal and instead he's one of the last decent people in the city. One of those who has never yelled even in the most private room of his own house; one who can live over your head as if he didn't exist. That's something they could say of me too: It's as if she weren't there. Slippers made of cloth, Your Honor. At most the toilet flushed before midnight.

She folded up the newspaper, leaving the photo of her old hero clearly in sight, and turned on her screen. Writing letters to judges already seemed a dumb thing to her. Worse than writing to the papers. What could she hope to get? They would laugh behind her back; they would treat her like an old crone. There never will be justice in this world. Her ideas began to be mixed up, and she preferred to start work, which she found simple and restful as always. Numbers are made in order to be mastered; it doesn't take genius to do it. Debits, management costs, reserves. All human inventions, made by us for us.

"Have you heard about Benzi?" Walter said in her ear just before eleven o'clock; he was all excited and had a conspiratorial air.

"Have you heard or haven't you?" he said again, a little more loudly.

"Who gives a damn, excuse me! Can't you see that I'm working on an account?" she answered with annoyance. And she didn't even try to patch it up; she let him go with his tail between his legs. She was losing track of the numbers and wanted to pick up the thread that had been broken. It didn't matter to her if she quarreled with Walter; nor did the car ride matter or the small saving she made. The winter was over and for the moment she didn't mind driving. She didn't have to feel bound to those two only because they drove better than she. She could retire and let them all go to the devil. Renata began to mutter a reproach and came in for her share. "Try not to butt in, if you don't mind!"

She liked the silence that followed upon her order. It was gratifying, that veiled rancor she felt all around her, those ugly words aimed unspoken at her: hysterical old woman, bootlicker, sellout. . . . She buried herself in the big numbers of a new product only recently distributed and already sold in the hundreds of thousands. Billions of lire, 2,723,000,000 plus change, to be exact. It's not true that numbers are all the same to an accountant. Big numbers filled her with pride, even if she knew that they owed nothing to her. The credit belonged to the foreign department, to the Commendatore who had sniffed out the deal, to the salesmen; she only did the numbers, but nevertheless she felt important. What an incredible head it took to grasp that a plastic trifle with four springs attached could provide food for hundreds of families, be represented in the huge numbers of a billing, could actually change the world, if only slightly. An insignificant little toy gave its tiny push to the great ball! While Bruno and she, and her father and mother, and Walter and Giancarlo could all turn to dust and disappear without anything being changed.

At about noon she finished her work and as usual took the summary sheets to the little professor, whom she found tired and swamped by papers in his father's office. He didn't care a hang for Luisa's numbers and glanced at them with outright annoyance. He was pale and gaunt, even his lips were faded. He was nothing but a boy, would never become a man.

"Well. . . ." he said indifferently, giving them back to her.

"The Commendatore has gone to take the baths?" she asked out of politeness.

"He left yesterday evening with my mother. Lucky him."

Luisa went back to her desk without even noticing Renata's presence; she was scratching her head, not knowing when it would be a good time to speak.

"We'd better not think about the sea, Luì!"

Luisa had only fleetingly caught sight of her microscopic little desktop beach, but her eyes had turned directly to the photo of her old hero. She imagined him in a dark cell, long and narrow, with his head in his hands, bathed in tears. Who knows if in prison, at least at night, there's a little quiet, or if it's all snoring or worse: outcries or bursts of laughter from young men.

She asked herself in alarm: This precious silence, once obtained, would it be better? Would things be changed? The silence she had asked for grew in her mind like a phantom taking on flesh. Soon it became a profound silence. Millions of kilometers of nothing around her. She tried to ask herself like a real scientist: What's happening to me in this sea of silence? There must be an answer! The only answer she could give was: It's hot. It's very hot, and one can't breathe. This was happening to her. Sweat ran down her chest and along her arms; her watchband burned her wrist, and the collar of her smock cut into her throat like a hemp rope.

"Are you feeling bad, Luì?" Renata was prompt to ask.

"I'm hot. I'm going to rinse myself off in the restroom. No, I'll go myself, thanks."

The restroom was empty, but she had to hurry. Soon the dumbbells from the secretaries' office would come in to brush their teeth and wash their underarms. She took off her glasses and bathed her face for a long time. Above the sink there was a high mirror that reached to the window; it was impossible not to see oneself. She was sure she must be red as a drunk, but she wasn't. She was sweating, but it wasn't visible. She was only pale. And the skin of her cheeks was dull and unhealthy. Her glasses had dug out a depression in the bone of her nose, and perhaps because of the lenses, the skin around her eyes had become thin and transparent. She would look like this, more or less, if she had just died.

For she was very sick. It was precisely in the company's restroom that she had to make such a discovery. What else were those continual swings of temperature if not the fits and starts of a motor that was dying; what else were those depressions, those fevers, those awful fears. Her wooden suit, as her father called it, was already being prepared. She imagined herself inside it, and looked at herself in the mirror as if she really saw it. Pallid, nailed between four wooden boards. Her hands rigid; her mouth half open in a grimace. In this extreme privacy she was surprised by the stupidest of the secretaries, who approached the sink swaying her hips as she did for the men.

"Hello," the girl said embarrassedly. Then she took hold of the eyelashes of her right eye and, without any reason, pulled them as if she wanted to pull them out.

"Hello," Luisa answered. She adjusted her hair with her fingertips and went back to her office.

"Are we going to lunch?" Renata asked with a little feigned smile, not wanting to overdramatize the situation.

"If you bring me a sandwich, I'll eat it."

"Is everything all right, boss?"

"Yes."

In the afternoon she told Giancarlo that she would be going home late, either by bus or with someone who had been delayed.

"For a couple of weeks it would be better if I take my own car," she said to him in the hall, "I'm always late." Seeing that Giancarlo said nothing, she added so as not to offend him, "That way I'll leave you a little more free, but be good."

At five she watched them leave: first, second, third, second, first. . . . She felt a profound sadness when the car of the companions she drove with disappeared around the corner of the body shop. The sun was still out; it was a mild, spring evening. The long trails of the airplanes and the small, low clouds on the horizon were a lovely pink. Even if she didn't look at them, she thought, they would still be lovely. She decided to wait for the driver who took the afternoon mail. She would accompany him as far as the station, and from there she would return home on foot, doing her shopping on the street. She hoped to find zucchini ready to put on the stove. After dinner there would be a science-fiction film on television. She thought about those things and did not pretend to be working. When the telephone rang, she answered a bit surprised. It was the little professor's secretary, who asked her to verify an account which, according to her, was grossly incorrect. Luisa turned on her computer with a gesture of defiance, getting herself ready to tell off that impertinent girl. She, grossly incorrect! And in the booking accounts! She immediately found the suspect page and checked it. There was a terrible mistake, one that not even Renata had ever made.

She took the corrected sheet to the girl who was waiting for her and could not succeed in appearing unconcerned. The girl, to relieve her embarrassment, said that even the biggest computers in the world sometimes made mistakes, but Luisa left without answering her and returned to her office. She went over the page with the mistake again and could find no explanation for it. The moment when she had typed that number had completely disappeared from her memory. Now that she had stopped checking the numbers, she contemplated them, feeling betrayed by them too. The porter was loading the mailbags and she followed him with her eyes trying to distract herself. Four bags, probably prizes for the children who had sent in their points. The calm face of the young man who was about to make the last trip of the day. Then he would shower and go out to enjoy himself with his friends. He seemed to her the type who played billiards, and he must be good at it. She opened the window a little, as far as she could, and called to him to wait for her. Then she hurried to take off her smock.

8

SHE DIDN'T LIKE TO TAKE SICK LEAVE JUST WHEN the Commendatore was not there. He would have called to ask her how she was and would have recommended rest, perhaps had his doctor visit her. Unfortunately, the old man was at the baths. She would have told him immediately that she had changed her mind about retirement. A brain that deals with numbers is more delicate than others; it takes almost nothing to compromise it. And she now forgot numbers of eight figures. It was an illness; there was nothing to do about it.

She had bought haphazardly a dozen or so magazines, as much as anything else in order to prevent herself from watching television all the time; during the day it made her melancholy. There were many articles about comets, well illustrated with photographs and large drawings. The passing of a comet was being expected then. She very attentively read an interview with a famous American astrophysicist who seemed a genius to her. He must have been a fascinating man, to judge by the photo. An easygoing gentleman in a checked shirt and well-pressed pants. On the other hand, articles about medicine irritated her. They were vanquishing everything, it was a matter of days, new frontiers, we are now in a position to, consider that formally. They were almost astonished when someone dared to complain: What's the matter, just because you don't have your behind anymore you're unhappy? Don't you like that nice little odorless bag, sterile and invisible, that collects feces outside the body? Luisa would willingly have done the astrophysicist's accounts, but the health experts seemed to her to be just blowhards. One particularly shameless article was called "Life Begins at Sixty." They're really peddlers of smoke, these health experts! And they can't even get rid of the common cold! Luì is not a fool, she said to herself proudly. Luì doesn't let herself be taken in. As her mother used to say: *Lisetta understands right off.*

She had arranged a cool, pleasant flow of air through the living room and out the wide open window of her bedroom. She enjoyed it seated in her armchair dressed in her large, blue men's pajamas. She had expected an attack of panic ever since she decided once and for all to retire, and instead she basked in a hitherto unknown idleness, sunny and peaceful. She was retiring, yes, but sooner or later everyone must. Her infirmities no longer allowed her to make the usual efforts; she needed rest and diet, and God's help.

She was preparing risotto with asparagus for dinner and could already smell them. The greengrocer had kept aside some beautiful asparagus for her. She piled the magazines on the floor and counted the months of notice that separated her from her pension. If they required her to stay for the entire period foreseen by the labor contract, she would be free at the end of September. Naturally, she would take more days of sick leave, and she expected unused vacation days to be counted. Her only duty now consisted in properly closing the accounts for which she was responsible. The rest of her work was always in perfect order, and there would be no need for a formal transfer of duties. What a blow for the Commendatore. What a disappointment. She couldn't look after him anymore. Their long collaboration was finished. She tried to choose carefully the words with which she would tell him she was leaving, but one phrase seemed too mawkish, another too arrogant, and she couldn't make up her mind. In the end, she decided to tell the head of personnel directly, without any fuss. Around noon she telephoned Renata. Out of fairness to the head of personnel, she divulged nothing of his decisions.

"Best wishes from the guys, too. They made a pilgrimage to your desk. They say that without you they're bored."

"They say, they say." She wanted to be more polite to Renata, but she didn't feel like joking.

"Well, how are you?"

"I feel a little tired. Did you see what I've worked out?"

"February in place of January, March in place of April." Renata couldn't control herself and started to laugh. It was her way of playing things down. "I think you had a bad fever. The lady came to work with a fever, she wants to be a hero of labor! Will you promise me that this time you'll take a few days off? The old man is on vacation; couldn't you stay at home for a week? Hey, it's not your factory."

"Yes, a week at least."

"And take care; go see a doctor and take some medicine and give me a call if I can help you with anything."

"I don't have any fever; I can go out."

She gave her the schedule for the most urgent jobs and returned to getting her meal. Cutting the asparagus, she coldly brought back to mind her mistakes. Perhaps in her body, without her being aware of it, a terrible battle was taking place against disease, and the brain had other things to do than follow its ordinary controls. The astrophysicist had said that the death of stars entailed an extraordinary event capable of overturning time. What did the dissolution of Luisa entail? Maybe nothing. She would become a ridiculous cardboard skeleton like her grandfather when they had exhumed him to put him in the ossuary. A shrunken monster of bone and cardboard. She had always liked making risotto because it helped her to think. Turning the wooden spoon was like walking or like rowing in a wide and peaceful river. She who had no close relatives or testamentary obligations beside her little apartment, how should she have prepared herself to become a little cardboard monster? But were her mother and father prepared? And all the others? The numberless mass of all the others? Billions and billions and billions. . . . They were all there already. If you're afraid of a place where you don't know anyone; and if instead they tell you: Listen, in the other room are your parents and grandparents. . . . If they tell you that because you must be afraid? Men go to pieces when they get sick; women are braver. Her mother maintained her grace even when she was vomiting green, and she never cried out. From the men's rooms infinite laments went up. No, Luisa would leave in her own way. She would never go into the filthy rooms of a hospital. She would rather kill herself. She didn't have to play a part for anyone. She was the absolute ruler of herself and she didn't intend to give up her command. Even thinking of her death, she behaved with the detachment of leaders who send others to die in their place. At the right time, she would kill herself with gas, she decided, tasting the risotto, and she would leave the house to the sisters' school, with the injunction always to keep the garden clean. If you think hard, you always find a solution.

The children had had their meal and they were playing and yelling in the sisters' garden. They kept her company.

They didn't annoy her at all. Nor did the lovers who kept apart near the low wall. They were a little pathetic, affected, but they didn't bother her. If nothing else, they were quiet. She liked the children, and she liked the calls of the sisters, who luckily were young and amused themselves together with the children.

She turned on the TV only when she brought the risotto to the table, smelling just as it should. The stories on the news program were at times quite exciting, but they did not supersede her attention to the risotto. If there had been men so monstrous as to invent the Resurrection, just imagine what the reality must be of news programs and magazines. Almost certainly those who appeared as saviors were in reality responsible for the evil they talked of fighting. Those who want to help us at all costs and pretend to be solicitous and sympathetic can never be distrusted enough. The cuts and mutilations of her mother's body, for example. That was how they had helped her. Tubes in her nose, needles in her veins, the catheter, sores left to putrefy.

Walter and Giancarlo didn't bother to telephone. How are you, when are you coming back, we'll stop by to pick you up, do you want anything from the store: things of that kind. Nothing. What's called restraint. Nevertheless, her meal was better than theirs. To bite into the asparagus with her teeth gives her an extremely refined pleasure. The smell of the asparagus, fleshy and metallic, blends perfectly with the aromas of the wine, even if it's wine diluted in a lot of water.

For half an hour there wasn't much traffic in the street. The short pause for the lunch hour. There were just a few young men in front of the bar talking almost normally. Luisa lit a cigarette and smoked it calmly. As a girl she had never played hooky from school, but if she could have felt then what she was feeling at this moment, she had missed something. In pajamas at two in the afternoon on a working day, with her legs drawn up on the couch and a cigarette between her fingers! She stretched comfortably and took away her plate. Then she came back to lie down on the couch. The canary went on for a long time giving its melodious answer to the sound of running water, and not to seem indifferent to him, she chimed in with a whistle. The slight wind caressed her gently; she was at peace, suffering neither from heat nor cold. Cars are passing somewhere; the barman is serving coffee; the gasoline attendant reopens the pump; the man dressed in blue goes into the bank. She was not in a hurry; on the contrary, she enjoyed her leisure, still relishing the smells of wine and asparagus. Only a vague anxiety, a nervousness born between her stomach and her heart, ran along her skin. The strange happiness of disobedience, the happiness of mischievous children. In reality she was not disobeying anyone; it was the change taking place too fast. An airplane roared, but it didn't appear in her square of sky. Then a youth loudly called someone five or six times while the others laughed. The wind became cooler, and Luisa thought that it was her ideal temperature. She had so many things to do and only a little anxiety in her chest. The Commendatore would call sooner or later. Walter too.

The old man called her in a dream soon afterward. From a Grand Hotel with an unpronounceable German name.

"My son told me you're not well."

"Yes, Commendatore." She wanted to tell him something else but couldn't. She smiled, even if no one could appreciate the effort it took. She reproached herself: perhaps she had smiled in too servile a manner. People used to bowing their heads. For millions of years. They didn't like it, but couldn't change it now for the better.

"Well, what's wrong?" the Commendatore asked, a little annoyed. Too much servility irritates the powerful. She should have known that too. And also too much timidity. The correct behavior is in the exact middle, on an invisible line. A tightrope walker's wire.

"I'm making mistakes. For some months I haven't felt well. I thought of retiring."

The old man said nothing. He didn't expect it. He was disappointed. A silence that had the strange shape of a black funnel, a small vortex.

"I don't have a particular sickness," Luisa tried to explain. "All I do is pant from the heat; I digest badly; my head is in the clouds."

"Nonsense." He snickered. "It's still some spark of youth. And what of me, getting colder all the time, what am I supposed to do? I put on woolen stockings and keep quiet. Undershirts with long sleeves, and underpants, until May. From October to May. You don't really believe that rubbish about the baths? I'm in a clinic where they warm your blood artificially. It takes plenty of dough."

"But then, it will get worse," she said in a tiny voice.

"Of course," he assured her wisely. "Everyone knows it, my poor Luisa. There's no pain worse than cold."

"I know," she admitted, feeling she was about to cry. Because she really was cold, and her shivers woke her up. She was half dressed on the couch, before a wide open window, and could hardly move for cold. She was barely able to move her arm to turn the pillows of the couch over on her body and slowly warm herself. It was night; she had slept for a long time.

The Commendatore would never call. He would shake her hand on the last day of work, would thank her as he did everyone, would give her his best wishes without getting up from his chair, without stopping to think even for a second about his own affairs. No one is as important as his affairs. Only his wife, perhaps. Despite everything she was quick to admire him. There are men with that talent in the blood, persevering men who are never distracted from their objectives. Does Signora Luisa want to leave? Good-bye and thanks. How many Signora Luisas have I seen sitting in his office, not even I can guess. No one is indispensable to the company.

Nor was the company indispensable to her, Luisa thought with pride, and she spent the rest of the night putting her future in order. With the meticulousness that everyone recognized in her. She was beginning a new phase and did not have a plan for it yet. She must do quickly what must be done, without waiting for tomorrow. A loafer's desk was always overflowing with paper; the desk of a good worker, on the other hand, was always clean and in perfect order. She had to write letters, turn in certificates, hunt for old documents. . . . By dawn she already had a first detailed list of the tasks that awaited her. At ten she went to visit her doctor, who, not having seen her for years, would not refuse her a certificate of illness; in fact, he wrote it with excessive conviction and also wrote a long prescription for medicines to help her. He advised her to make an immediate appointment with a well-known specialist, and she took down the address and telephone number without protesting. The doctor wrote a long letter for her to take along and gave it to her in an envelope together with the prescription. She needed a complete examination; she had been rather naughty not to have been examined for so many years. Yes, he assured her, she must make an appointment as soon as possible. Of course, she didn't feel too poorly. Thank you, thank you! Good-bye! She went out of the doctor's office and, as she had planned beforehand, went to wait for a number 47 bus that passed nearby. She had more important things to do than waste time in clinics and pharmacies like the pensioners who vegetated in waiting rooms, loaded with tests and X rays, engrossed in the comparison of their red corpuscles. Cowards. They crept along; she walked with head high.

The end of the line for the number 47 was the municipal cemetery, and several seats were taken by old people carrying flowers bought at the market. Luisa had no flowers; it was not her purpose to visit her relatives. She had decided to buy a burial niche and wanted to choose one carefully. They had told her on the phone that she had several choices. It was not an urgent matter, but she had never thought of it before and she must now think of it. Perhaps there was a dash of magic in all this, she admitted to herself, smiling: preparing for the worst one lives longer.

She made a very old man her guide; working there, he found it normal that someone should come to pick out a burial site. He seemed truly convinced about the new section of the cemetery, which Luisa, to begin with, didn't even want to see. It was far from the gate, on the other side of the hill; she had never happened to go there. After they had passed through two or three lanes, the new chapels appeared beyond a long hedge in a semicircle facing a meadow. On the right, in small blocks, the most economical arrangements, but still of very decent quality. Four or five levels at most. They resembled the houses on the lower parts of the hills; they were not villas, but they could be called small luxury buildings.

There were still only a few permanent guests, but there were many reservations, especially for the family chapels; a few transfers were expected among deceased who were abandoning old chapels now smothered by the immense constructions of the last thirty years, ugly buildings of twenty levels already full of cracks. The guide confided to her, "In five years they will all be taken." Her initial mistrust overcome, Luisa began to find the place to her taste. But she shouldn't let herself be influenced, when one buys something, one must weigh every detail calmly. The road was far away, and behind the new surrounding wall could be seen a beautiful field of grain. She went up a short flight of stairs, already embellished with a fragrant hedge. Even the metal handrail had been carefully chosen, and the marble steps were not lacking strips to prevent slipping. Seen at close range, the ordinary fittings, lamps and photograph holders, were even elegant, without fake tongues of flame or weeping angels. She liked the last block of three levels on the right, the nearest to the wall. It had a bigger porch than the others, and the view, if it made sense to be concerned about it, ranged beyond the walled-in field and took in a large modern quarter. "These four are sold," the man said right away so that she wouldn't choose uselessly. On the left there was only one occupant. A young woman dead at thirty, dark haired, with a beautiful, sincere smile; the photograph had been taken in the open, in a big garden. It must have been spring; she was wearing a light cotton dress, turquoise colored. She had been dead barely four months. What an attractive girl; nothing like that boiled fish, her niece. She would be an excellent neighbor. "I'll take that one above," she said to the man, who approved in silence. It seemed as if he wanted to tell her: Don't be concerned about my treating you well; you can die in peace. "It's seven hundred and fourteen block B," he said, pronouncing every syllable. And Luisa took note, writing on the back of the prescription that she would never use. "It's a bit of a walk," the man said as they returned to the main gate, "but one doesn't come here to take walks." Luisa smiled and looked around. The scent of cypresses was delightful, and the bright sky was full of joyful swallows. Seated behind a minute desk, the man prepared documents to be taken to City Hall, and as he wrote he started to talk to her in dialect about politics, and she answered in the same, pleased to be treated like an old citizen. "Men are always complaining about the governments; women say they're all the same." "Believe me, dear lady," said the man, "not even the dead are all the same." And handing her the papers, he confided to her his theory of how a cemetery ought to be. Nothing more than a large common hole at the bottom of a wall, into which the corpse wrapped in a sheet is slipped. On the other side of the wall, invisible, would be the furnace. All the ashes would then be mixed and used to fertilize flowers and plants. If they wish, the relatives come to the wall to weep, or they put in notes to the dead as the Jews do at the Wailing Wall. The caretakers would collect the notes and take care of the flowers. And perhaps keep a public record, maybe on a computer. Cremated on this spot on X day of Y year. "But since there is no crematorium wall," Luisa asked, "what sort of coffin do you advise?"

"The one that costs least," the man said unhesitatingly, "the coffin is of no importance whatever; it's an absolute swindle. You might as well throw away your savings at the movies or in the South Seas."

The world is full of wise men who go unheard, Luisa thought on her way back to the bus stop. In various parts of the city, perhaps every day, ingenious ideas appear that together could change the world.

There was no bus at the bus stop. An old woman was looking at her from a flower stall, and Luisa approached to pass the time. She didn't offer much choice, but the flowers she had were beautiful. Luisa suddenly felt guilty; the graves of her parents were near at hand, and she had not visited them for months. She bought a handsome bouquet and hurried toward a secondary entrance that allowed her to go around most of the monumental section. She didn't have to cover more than a hundred meters, but the weight of the water and the awkward container with a hole in which she had to carry it made her sweat. Her father's vault was dusty and bare. Luisa cleaned it with a paper handkerchief, then arranged the flowers which were really magnificent. The picture of her father was old-fashioned, and for that very reason she liked it more than most of the others. Well-trimmed mustaches, slightly long sideburns, a gray jacket, and buttoned shirt without a tie. A firm and honest look, more like a captain of *bersaglieri* than an employee of the post office. Her mother's vault was ten meters away, on the third level. She cleaned off the memorial tablet and the photograph and placed the remaining flowers. Then she said the Our Father and hurried back to the bus stop. She was just in time to board the number 47, which was already closing its doors. She sat down in the last row and turned to look at the cemetery: its long lines of cypresses, the flower shops that crowded around it. What a strange place, she thought. A cemetery is at the same time the most sacred and the most insignificant place in the world. Mummies, cardboard dolls. Over these poor remains the Lord of the Apocalypse and of infinite pity was supposed to rule. Among human beings there was no similar pity. Luisa closed her eyes and imagined the perfumed white cloak of the Powerful Unknown One, full of compassion, who takes back to himself all that is his. Even the hairs of your head are counted in heaven, every bit of your wretched excrement, every drop of saliva, every drop of blood.

She reached City Hall a little out of breath, but no sooner had she signed the check and given it to the clerk than she felt herself in excellent humor again. Usually when she encountered public employees whom she considered ignorant and uncouth, she remained irritated for hours and imagined inflamed speeches directed to the mayor and to the city. Now she had no need for them. Now her brain could let itself go: she had thought of almost everything. The really important accounts were closed. She had about forty million

lire left, and of course the house, plus a few small invest-
ments, and then her pension, which although modest, could
suffice her.

The bar in front of the cathedral had tables outside, and it
seemed a good idea to buy a newspaper, sit down in the
shade, and drink something. She ordered a cappuccino and
began to read the local news. There was only a brief mention
of her assassin hero in the announcement of the young man's
funeral. She looked at the youths coming and going around
her on motorbikes or on foot and didn't find them too disagreeable; they were better in the morning, she thought, perhaps the meaner whelps were still sleeping. In the paper she
found news of two fatal accidents: two boys on a motorcycle, and an old man fallen into a ditch in his car. Who knows
if one of them might end up in the new section of the
cemetery. Pigeons rummaged among the tables; a faint and
not unpleasant odor of asphalt hung in the air. The sun beat
down on the cathedral and made it shine. The large plants set
in pots also shone, and so did the flowers that surrounded
the space of the bar, cyclamen and red and white geraniums.

She paid for the cappuccino and started on foot toward
home, stopping to rest in a couple of stores she liked. When
she reached home, there were two packages of gifts: several
films on cassette and some mysteries of Maigret and Nero
Wolfe. After lunch, she began to read a mystery, but she had
difficulty remembering the names of the characters and had
continually to go back to the table of contents. She was only
able to follow the meals and the descriptions of the crimes.
After an hour, she tired of reading and turned on the television. She had to accustom herself to reading again; she felt
like seeing a bit of gymnastics. For a long time she watched a
psychic who was being consulted over the telephone. She
was a woman of her own age who perhaps believed in her
tarot cards, but to Luisa she looked more than anything else

like a cunning old fox, ready to pry information out of her clients. There's been a loss, I know there has, and almost tears from the other end. Yes, it's true, there has been, very important to me. Too easy, Luisa thought; when a poor women is reduced to calling up a psychic, she's lost something for sure. Every now and then, however, the woman got annoyed, and not always in a banal way. Let him go, she was advising a girl with a trembling voice; it's an affair that's not working. Are you serious? Yes, it's best to speak plainly. There are other women, other interests, you're only a sort of plaything. You'll see nothing else from him: betrayal, loss of money, even serious personal dangers. Does he drive fast? Then let him go once and for all. Someone will die with him, if you really want to know; he's a man who brings harm, even if he himself escapes. There it is. The devil. Death. Ciao, my girl. Be on guard. Another telephone call. Hello?

The devil's card appeared again on television, and this time Luisa was frightened. She imagined him naked and sweating, with bloodshot eyes, black curls glued by sweat around two small, pointed horns. Not with hooves but with most beautiful hands, and surrounded by the light of a fire. A devil of thirty years, who naturally resembled Bruno. His sex, too, dangling before him, was fiery red and made him look ridiculous. How could she be frightened by a devil dressed up like Bruno? She recalled a confidence of her cousin, who continued to suffer the frequent sexual assaults of her husband against her wishes. I'm dry, she had said, it's like putting it into a beefsteak. An expression that had astonished her, because it wasn't part of her habitual language. Probably her cousin hoped to gain the house for her daughter with her visits and friendship as the last remaining relative. Nothing was easier. But she was wrong to hope so. Luisa took a sheet of paper and began to write: by her own will and fully aware, etc., her apartment situated in via, etc., she bequeathed to the

Sisters of the Sacred Heart, who, however, could sell it only to beautify or in other ways improve, and especially keep clean, their kindergarten in via, etc., under her windows. Of her remaining bank accounts, she ordered that they be divided equally between her cousin and the sisters, after the expenses of her funeral had been paid. In that regard, she wanted only a simple coffin of beechwood and ordered that it be moved by municipal coach, without flowers, to her property number, etc., at the municipal cemetery, etc.

She reread twice what she had written and then signed it. It was the first day she had dedicated entirely to herself, and she had already signed a heap of papers. She had also taken flowers to her parents. Yes, she was working well. In order to make much less important decisions, Renata and Walter worried and complained for months. She raised the volume of the television and put her house in order. Then she started to iron. She didn't dislike ironing, sometimes it relaxed her, but now she ought to do it early in the morning when it was cool, or in the evening. She ironed for ten minutes and was bathed in sweat. Even though she was uncomfortable, she continued to iron in her slip. She had set up the board in the middle of the living room at the best ventilated spot in the house, and to make it easier for the air to move she had blocked the doors with chairs. But if the breeze was warm, how could it cool her off? It was a city breeze, smelling of dust and gasoline and even burnt rubber. To be certain, she smelled the iron, but the odor did not come from it.

The weeks she still had to spend at the company did nothing but accentuate her detachment, also because she had decided to go to work alone, in her own car. The Commendatore, who had returned from taking the cure, was always in a bad mood and sulked toward her. When they met, she greeted him first, but he limited himself to muttering something without looking at her. The little professor, on the other hand, always greeted her now and sometimes smiled with his little muzzle of a white rabbit, perhaps because she had dared defy his father's will. Luisa had always thought that saying good-bye at work would be a terrible moment, but it was not like that. One day she even saw with a different eye the little beach on her desk, the white shells and the sand she had touched so often with the tips of her fingers. Her beach was a ridiculous piece of junk. She turned the big ashtray that contained it in her fingers, and threw it in the wastebasket.

She made no more errors in her accounts, even when she had to take on a great accumulation of back work. What weighed on her most was the trip going and coming and conversations with her colleagues, who only talked about her pension. By now the company was nothing but a goods shed like all the others, and the Commendatore and the heads seemed insignificant to her. The sample room, which she had always found sinister, now nauseated her, and unfortunately the greater part of her colleagues also caused the same reflex. When Renata spoke to her, she avoided looking at her, and even if she didn't see her, the unpleasant smell she gave off made her stomach turn.

Just at that time the Commendatore took on a new high-level employee, a young woman who had a degree in literature but now occupied herself with marketing. She had an ugly mouth and was rather fat; she thought she was beautiful but oozed vulgarity at every pore. Luisa saw her often going through the hallways with a container of yogurt in her hand; when she met someone she laughed loudly, bringing a couple of spoonfuls to her lips, which she then neglected to clean. Thus, when she spoke, she sprayed yogurt on her interlocutors, and a little white slaver formed in the corners of her mouth. Luisa had received her very coldly, and the other women responded by ignoring her. In any case, this new employee was too busy with her continual visits to the executives; she passed from one head to another, swaying on her huge behind, carrying proudly ever more heavy files. It was enough for Luisa to look at her to know she wouldn't last long.

Perhaps in order to make room for the new arrival, Luisa's last two months of work were remitted, and she was free before the summer vacation.

"Best wishes and thanks," the Commendatore said to her before answering the telephone. He held out his hand like an important prelate, without getting up and answering "Hello" in a barely audible voice.

"Best wishes to you, too," she answered, turning gaily on her heels.

Then she went down the executives' stairway with a bag packed with her personal things and attached a card to the notice board for her colleagues who were already at lunch: GOOD-BYE TO ALL, LUISA.

She had told Renata she would leave without saying good-bye. For the others, a card would suffice. Before turning right at the exit from the lot, she looked at the company in her mirror and tried to think of how she felt. She was tense; her heart was beating strongly, and she smiled nervously. I'm satisfied, she thought, stepping on the accelerator, and turned into the road home whistling softly.

9

WHEN RENATA TELEPHONED HER FROM THE OF-
fice, Luisa didn't know what to say. She pretended
to be interested in her gossip but really was bored
by it and not provoked to any nostalgia. And she
instantly forgot the rather excessive compliments
that Renata had perhaps enhanced with something
of her own. The best accountant. An honest person.
Such a beautiful lady. High-sounding words that
people say when they have nothing to say. Faces,
rooms, toys, streets known for so many years were
fading in her day by day, without leaving a trace.
Even Renata, who had cried at the moment of saying good-bye, even Renata would soon be forgotten.

The void left by work made itself felt especially
through her body. At a certain point in the morning, between nine and ten o'clock, she would find
herself seated at the dining table, her arms crossed
and her eyes lost in the void. Her body continued
to seat itself at a desk, and her eyes looked in vain

for a computer screen. And her fingers seemed to be or-
phaned from their keyboard and didn't know what to do
with themselves. As soon as Luisa became aware of this, she
got up and went to lie down on the couch, and there she
stretched, yawned, and moved her toes. Thirty-five years are
a whole life. A period of detoxification was needed, and not
only for her stomach. If her stomach could be cured with a
diet, the rest of her body needed some recreation and new
interests and, naturally, open air and sunshine. She therefore
tried to get herself into the habit of going to the park every
morning if it wasn't raining and she felt well. The fever,
which she had decided to ignore, came back only in the afternoon. Around ten o'clock, she stuck a mystery or a magazine into her purse and walked calmly to the park. She never
met old people, only students and mothers with their car-
riages. The students, almost all from the university, either
studied or slept; the mothers, on the other hand, read magazines and rocked their babies, each with her own particular
rhythm. If the babies cried, the mothers went back and forth
for a little while or picked them up and showed them the
goslings and the swans. One day she became aware that there
were few mothers with children out walking. They were all
at home working, busy with their bits of plastic and screws,
their business letters. What a shame, she thought, what a loss.

She couldn't endure more than a couple of hours in the
park. It embarrassed her to read and feel herself continually
looked at, even if in reality no one looked at her in any special way. To be among others takes a great effort; at a certain
point she wants to go home and take off her shoes and dress
and put on something really comfortable. She also would
have liked to close the door to all the noises of the young
men, but these came in from every side; they invaded the
house, the ears, the brain. You don't see them, but they're always around you, and they remind you that you don't have

She waited on the terrace for ten more minutes, but nothing happened. The furious motorcyclist was swallowed up by the crowd of young men, and everything returned to what it had been before. A little disappointed, she went back in the house and decided to watch *E.T.*, even though by now she knew all the funny lines by heart and the puppet no longer moved her. After a quarter of an hour, she admitted she was bored. It wasn't even ten-thirty. She dressed and went out to get an ice cream. There was a small kiosk opposite the main gate of the park. Passing among the youths, she found them almost normal; it seemed reasonable that everyone would want to be out in the open on a beautiful evening like this one. Maybe it had been a mistake to drop the nails. She had been too angry and lost control. After all, it was summer.

The streetlights didn't allow her to see the sky; it must be full of stars and somewhere in it, surely, there was a big moon. The air was cool, and the thoughts that came to her were clear and sensible. As she ate the ice cream, she thought her life had still to acquire a rhythm. She was living as though she were on vacation, and instead this was her new life. She needed habits, schedules: Thursday, the movies; Sunday, the country with her cousin; Monday, the laundry; Tuesday, the ironing; get up at eight, shop at nine, read at three. . . . The waitress who had brought the ice cream and now showed her the bill was very nice; she left her a small tip and struck out in the direction opposite the one to her house. Planning future days relaxed her. At the intersection, rather than head up toward the hill, she took a central street that led to her original neighborhood. She enjoyed recognizing the old stores, the newsstand, a sign that had survived and was now exhibited like an antique. In the place of an elegant dress shop, there had been an unpretentious dressmaker's saturated with fumes. Her father met his best friends there, behind a thick curtain that smelled of smoke. And up there, at the top of the steps, was the old prison. She climbed the steps and found the stone tablet still there.

Here, her father had told her, pointing to the tablet which was already almost illegible, the anarchists were shot. The last decent Italians. One of them was a close friend of your grandfather, who was a socialist, and in fact look closely, right at the top: he had the same name as mine. Only the last line could be read now: Assassinated by royal bullets. At that moment a crowd was coming out of the movie house, and she observed sadly that none raised their eyes toward the plaque for the poor anarchists assassinated by royal bullets. Assassin or incompetent kings, thieving owners! Only her father knew the truth of the world. And he went on ahead with his hands clasped behind his back.

That's the race from which my father comes, she said to herself full of pride. From the great heroes of history. Spartacus with the face of Kirk Douglas, Garibaldi, Karl Marx, Errico Malatesta. She didn't remember history at all anymore, not the Punic Wars, nor the outbreak of the First World War, and not even the dead caused by the Second. A million, perhaps two. She thought that the dead were modest, they weren't displeased to be forgotten, they leave you alone. You can forget the anniversary of their death and never visit them, without giving offense.

It was hard to walk on the flagstones. She felt her calves beginning to hurt. When she started to sweat again, she stopped and pretended to be interested in an old doorway, a dusty little Madonna, even an automobile. If there was nothing actually to look at, she stared at her watch or looked at the sky as if she expected the arrival of a spaceship. Coming out of a dark alley, she became aware of having lost her way. She didn't know which way to go. She walked at hazard for a little while without becoming alarmed. She recognized particular buildings, doorways, stores, but together they formed an unknown street. After a few minutes, she came out into a familiar, small square where she had played as a child, and the city recovered its usual aspect. When the anxiety of being lost had completely passed, she thought that it had been a good feeling, perhaps frightening when she was living it, but good when she found herself again after being lost.

She went home through the center of town, arriving in the old market square. Youths were swarming around the nightclub, and many more were pouring out of the bars in the area. Long lines of motorcycles, cars crowded into parking spaces, various kinds of music all mixed together. When she reached her house, she saw that the nails were gone, and the faces of the young men looked no different than usual. In the elevator she felt a pleasant shiver of cold. She pulled her cotton jacket tight and rubbed her arms. Tiredness helps one forget, it's like a medicine. She closed the shutters and windows, pulled the curtains, and fell asleep almost immediately.

The next day she heard that a nail had stuck into the foot of one of the youths. The news vendor said they were themselves responsible; it was some sort of quarrel between gangs, and they were throwing handfuls of nails. Nails were just what they needed, as if the pissing wasn't enough, if he could take the liberty of speaking so. Luisa answered by shaking her head and smiling. She hadn't accomplished a big gesture, when you got right down to it. She had to keep a careful watch on her nerves and stick to the plans decided upon. Among these were some important reading projects. She had already read, albeit with many difficulties, two complete chapters of a gigantic manual of general economics. Today she was going to begin reading the Bible. Even though it had belonged to her mother, she had never opened it and didn't know how to approach it. She remembered only the episodes of the Gospels she had been told as a child. By chance she opened to the Gospel of St. John, and she plunged into reading it, not omitting a single note of commentary. She read it and reread it, taking down the most important phrases in a notebook.

She took special note of the names of two places: the brook Kedron and the hill of the Skull, Golgotha in Hebrew. She imagined with many details these two places so crucial to all that happened. She saw the palms, the moon, the long black clouds, squads of Roman soldiers moving in the dim light, wagons pulled by a horse, small whitewashed houses. Those places exist, no doubt of it. It gave her an odd excitement to think about such old stories. Two thousand years. She tried to think of that much time by putting twenty men of a hundred years in a row. They weren't so many. At the cemetery she had seen the tomb of a man who had died at one hundred three years. Twenty tombs of centenarians, and one sank into that distant past. The brook Kedron, Golgotha, the poor white houses, the desert. One can't consider a time corresponding to twenty tombs as excessive. But people who had been able to invent the beautiful story of E. T., couldn't they have invented some other story? She read over and over a line from one of her notes: "It is he, the disciple, who bears witness to these things, and has written them." And just as when she put her finger on a number from which she was capable of determining an infinity of others, she decided that this was the center of the book. And face-to-face with this center, her father, and in the end her mother too in the San Francesco clinic, had frowned and said no. They did not believe. Unfortunately, they did not believe. "If you don't believe in me, believe in my works." But which works? They were just words.

She must think about it calmly, not settle the whole question in an instant. Religious doubts stimulate the brain like a difficult calculation. One had to know the texts really well, she said to herself with scientific scruple, before forming a personal opinion. She turned on the radio and decided to wash the windows even though it was dark. She felt good and wanted to take advantage of it. She had washed the shutters recently, and they were still quite clean. From her folding steps she could see almost the whole street, full of motorcycles and young men. The sound of the ball never stopped day and night. She tried to ignore it and went on thinking of the deserts where immaculate angels appeared, or the most cunning liars. In that time the deserts swarmed with angels; they went into houses and tombs, flew above the dunes, kept company with the saints. Perhaps only the souls of unborn children are really angels, pure as the cool wind that cleans the sky above the park and dries one's sweat. She put the cloth into the basin and fell into thought: I ask in your name to see one of your angels at least once, even if only for a second. She looked into the corners of the room, at her furniture, around the lights of the lamps. She would have been satisfied with an angel as big as a doll. The angel did not appear, and Luisa felt herself alone. Now she asked to see her father and mother again, but she did not see them. It must have been her fault. Perhaps she didn't feel their absence anymore; or rather she felt a strange relief at knowing they were gone from the scene. It made her feel more free. By now they would be old and sick and humiliated by their need for care. Luckily, she was alone and could think about important things. A cross upon a skull, the Son of man raised above the peoples. And when he returns to summon us, he will fill all the space of the sky. An old muddy street came to her mind. Two naked feet that proceeded with effort through the mire; and then stone houses and little kitchens lit by candle ends and old lamps. She sensed the smell of her past in her nose, of humidity and the earth. Then she became aware that the humidity was increasing, that she was finding it hard to breathe, and her head was turning. She hurried to get down from the ladder, but in her haste she missed the last step and fell forward, turning the basin of water over onto the carpet. With trembling hands she immediately felt her arms and legs to see if anything was broken. Luckily, she had not harmed herself; there were small pains here and there at her knees and a wrist, a tingling throughout her body.

She sat up on the rug and laughed at the danger she had escaped. She thought the most beautiful phrase she had read in the afternoon was the one that described Jesus before the body of Lazarus: "Jesus wept." How could anyone lie about an event like that? She continued to think about it, while a soccer game had started up in front of the garages, with many spectators, and the uproar was unbearable.

The sound of the ball drumming in the courtyard would be the ground note of her summer; she must resign herself. The number of youths grew from one evening to the next. Luisa tried to count them and got as far as two hundred, but since they were continually moving from one sidewalk to the other, she had to give it up. There must have been at least five hundred. The ball bounced against the wall every twenty or thirty seconds. Then someone screamed with joy because the wall of the garages was their goal. To keep herself from getting angry, she decided to look at the photos that had been thrown confusedly into the chest of drawers in the lit-tle bedroom. She was curious to look at the same pictures Bruno had seen when he was searching for the one with the pike. The uppermost layer of the chest was almost com-pletely made up of photos of the trip to Greece. Their real honeymoon, taken two years before they were married. Their great sexual passion. They spent most of the time in their room. There in the bungalow behind the straw um-brella. The ferry, her first foreign country. The live lobster, the pierced grouper in its death throes, the fish grilled with herbs. Do whatever you want to me! she had cried out to him during a burning embrace. Do whatever you want to me! It seemed funny to her, but she had really cried it out, with that happy face captured forever in the portraits, and who knows how many tourists had heard her.

Then she dug among the older pictures. She with her mother, her first dress, confirmation, she and her mother and father on bicycles. The steps of the sisters. Her parents' wedding. Just before she had cried out to herself, Do whatever you want to me! and now she was almost in tears. Who knows if her father had seen her even on those summer days there in Greece. The dead see everything and are not shocked. Like us when we see cats coupling. A summer frenzy that safeguards the species. The dead look on with a detachment that does not make us feel ashamed. I assume that they look on. Men and women who eat and move their bowels, a fine spectacle. She took the picture of her parents' wedding and went to place it on the credenza in the living room. Sooner or later she must have it framed; it made her sad that it was so limp. She lit a fire under the meat rolls and went back to look at the picture. Her father was too thin and her mother had the shadow of a mustache. Their clothes, ugly and stiff, seemed to have been cut with a hatchet and must have been heavy as blankets.

SUMMER PROGRESSED AND THE HEAT became asphyxiating. Luisa woke early when the city was still asleep and had her breakfast in front of the wide open window in the pink and blue dawn. Only the swallows were awake, darting silently in wide circles. The serene dawn, which she observed with pleasure, was also a portent of the heat to come, which in fact exploded by seven o'clock. She went for a walk earlier and earlier, when the municipal sanitation trucks and those for milk delivery were the only ones moving in the streets, and she returned soon to take shelter at home, where she could pull off her clothes and shower as often as she wanted to. She bought a portable air conditioner, which she turned on only at the hottest times of day because it gave her a headache. Her old fan was kept turned on in front of her armchair until evening. She ironed now only before the sun came up, listening to a program for truck drivers on the radio. She was almost never able to stick to the schedule she had laid down. She ate without appetite and only after sunset. And she read a lot, especially the mysteries of Nero Wolfe, and watched the television news, with great interest when something sensational was happening like wars or massacres, and with profound sadness when all they did was talk about politics. If two armies were facing one another, and if military planes were taking off, then her day had a good beginning.

She didn't like to see images of people fleeing, of children wounded and starving, of young soldiers lined up on the ground, but everyone has his own battle to fight. She had hers against boredom, which on certain days made her suffer as much as the heat and the noise. She still read the Gospels and scraps from the Old Testament, though she usually didn't like them. The creation of the world, Adam and Eve, the Pharaoh: fairy tales for grown-ups, inexplicable whims of God. Build me an altar of acacia wood covered with pure gold, and let the fuel of the lamps be of pure olive oil, and of fine, twisted linen the garments of the priests, of purple, violet, and scarlet. . . . Minutely rendered details, that was a great part of the Bible. A continual putting one's trust in God, and never any answers to man's questions. She had not robbed, nor fornicated, nor told falsehoods: from the point of view of the laws, she was up to the mark. But that wasn't why she could consider herself without sin. She didn't make love to anyone because she didn't desire to, and she didn't rob because theft was contrary to her nature. After a bit of sacred reading, she turned to Nero Wolfe. She had discovered that it was possible to read mysteries without understanding everything. She immersed herself in the reading and succeeded in forgetting the heat for a while. She alternated two light cotton dresses, full and unpretentious, two sacks almost, but sometimes she felt herself suffocating all the same. In the middle hours of the day the heat made her pant. She drank a great deal of cold water, which, however, could not cool the source of her heat that was born in her heart and irradiated her chest, stopping just below the skin that was being cooled by the air conditioner. And the new mole, probably irritated by the rubbing of her brassiere, had swollen and caused her a continual and irresistible itch.

To escape the heat while not paying the prices of the high season, she made a reservation at her usual small hotel at the shore. She would have liked to leave immediately, but the owner told her that they were late doing repairs. So she took the advice of her news vendor and signed up to take swimming lessons for retirees at the municipal pool. To be sure, she didn't really need lessons, but that was the most economical way of using the pool every day. When the heat became unbearable toward midday, she went out with her big sports bag and remained away until six at least. Between one dip and the next, she ate a pizza or an ice cream, drank something cold, and especially read magazines. As soon as she felt hot again, she went back and immersed herself. She didn't swim much, in part not to lose in the water the plaster that covered her ugly mole. She stayed on her feet most of the time and walked slowly from one side to the other of the pool. She struck up an acquaintance with a lady of her age, a blonde still in very good form, and from time to time they talked about the articles they read in the magazines, or about the heat and the hole in the ozone layer. Her name was Laura; she owned a small hotel that had been rented out for years, and she had a passion for painting. One of those supple and agile women that a man would call sinuous. Luisa had noticed her precisely because of her graceful way of moving. And then she had observed her attentively, and one day answered with a smile to her greeting. What a vital woman, both cheerful and melancholy at the same time and in the right measure. She must have been a very beautiful woman, and at bottom still was. Only a woman is able to see the beautiful girl hidden in the body grown heavy of another woman. Too bad. She saw it very well.

One day they left the pool together and went to Laura's house to look at her pictures. She, too, lived in the center, and she shared a place with her daughter, a girl of twenty-five. It was a big, old apartment, well preserved, that occupied the top two floors of a hotel Luisa had never noticed before. The canvases were piled up by the dozens in a huge room with three windows. Laura painted only flowers in full bloom, from small bunches of wild flowers to large compositions of magnificent exotics. All rendered with bold brush strokes and lavish color. Luisa knew nothing about painting, but they seemed to her very beautiful, and her compliments were sincere. In a corner, in a big wooden frame, she noticed a photograph of a man, and Laura, laughing, introduced her to her husband.

"Unfortunately, it's true they don't live as long," she said as she served the iced tea. "I heard a scientist tell about that; it's not just silly talk. . . ."

Then they spoke of the noises in the center, of the traffic and motorcycles, unbearable when the windows were left open, and of the pension at the shore where Luisa would be going in a few days.

"When I worked, I couldn't wait to leave for the sea. Now I'm going almost out of duty. It must be that I'm not very well."

Before she left, Laura pressed her to accept a small painting, a beautiful bunch of violets, which she wrapped in two sheets of newspaper. She said that she would return the visit, and she seemed sincere.

Luisa went home carrying her beautiful violets with exaggerated care, happy as a child who has received an unexpected gift. She immediately hung it above the couch, on the most important wall of her house, and made sure that it could be seen well even from the entrance. She spent at least an hour contemplating her only painting from near and far, appreciating particularly two large drops of violet oozing from a petal, which gave the impression of wanting to color the grass of the meadow. She liked that wealth of color, the vitality it expressed, the same vitality that radiated from Laura's bright eyes. She kept repeating: What a beautiful painting, what a beautiful lady, what a beautiful neighbor.

Three days later she left for the shore, even though she no longer had much desire to go there. The evening hours that she preferred were spoiled by a new volleyball court that was kept open until dinner time. And the hotel's famous fried fish had become greasy and soggy and remained for the most part on her plate.

After a week of migraines and stomachaches, she invented a relative's illness and went home, to be benevolently welcomed by a magnificent thunderstorm full of lightning bolts. She enjoyed seeing her canary again, who had been cared for, as in previous summers, by Giancarlo's aunt, a pleasant lady who was passionately given to raising dozens of canaries. Bringing it home in the midst of the storm, she whistled all the way to welcome and encourage it. When she carried it in the car, she put the cage on the right seat and secured it with the seat belt, but the bird began to sing only when it was home, next to the festive water Luisa left running for it. "Welcome back," she said, giving it some cuttlefish bone.

She had done well to come home. The tenants of the garret apartment were away at the seashore, and the youths at the bar also seemed thinned out and less noisy than usual. The thunderstorm that welcomed her was followed by others and the temperature for a few days stayed bearable. Only in the mornings did she continue to feel unwell, a gift of the bad meals she had ingested at the shore. When the heat returned, she again frequented the pool, but Laura was not to be seen, and she did not find other companions. The usual elderly, the sick, the depressed. The victims of summer.

10

SHE SLIPPED INTO FALL, THEN WINTER, ALMOST without noticing them. The weeks passed idle and unvarying, and she felt no dissatisfaction. On rainy days she went out only to do the necessary shopping: three or four bags at most and a few magazines.

After the rains came the fog, and soon after the frost of an intensely cold January. Poor souls who had to go out early in order to get to work. She, too, had gone out thousands of times when it was still dark, and she didn't have to feel sorry for the others. If she woke up very early, she thought of Walter and Giancarlo who were heading sleepily toward the highway, or she imagined Renata being late, with her shoes, hat, and gloves all of the same color, and she could almost hear her grumbling. It was strange to spend these winter mornings at home, waiting under the covers for the sun to come up, listening to the radio and munching on almond cookies. She enjoyed the warmth and her comforts, but she never succeeded in feeling completely rested. Even when she slept for a long time, she always woke with the disagreeable sensation of not having slept enough. If she had rested for a few more minutes, she would have felt perfect. In the morning, despite the sugar in her cookies, she continued to feel weak. Now and then she would close her eyes and listen to the dull hum of unfulfilled sleep. She wasn't tired enough to sleep, and she didn't have the energy to get out of bed. Still, she could live with weakness; after all, she had nothing to do, and it would have been a pleasant enough January if she hadn't noticed by chance one afternoon that the glands in her armpits were swollen. She had been looking at Laura's violets for a long time and had put her hands under her arms to warm them. From close up they weren't violets but purple brush strokes placed by chance on top of green brush strokes, which were superimposed in turn on brown strokes. In sum, a trick. And just as she was reflecting on the falsity of the violets, her fingers discovered the glands.

She did not feel anguish, nor did she rebel; only her lips curved downward and she felt disappointed. She stood for a long time almost hypnotized by the painting, her eyes on the violets and arms crossed on her breast, her fingers intent upon analyzing each of the enlarged glands. It was like sliding her fingers into a pigeon's nest full of eggs. She had covered the mole with a plaster and did not think of it anymore, but what could she do about the glands?

She remembered the appointment set by her doctor, but it was obvious that she wouldn't go. She didn't even have to make a decision about that. It took courage to put your faith in their treatments, or you had to be ignorant, someone without experience. She had seen her father suffer, and her mother; she had seen too much. If she had to go, she would go; if she didn't have to go, it would only hasten her going.

And if by now there was no reason for hoping that she might be cured, she had to admit it. These glands were too repulsive. She really wouldn't be able to show them to her doctor; in fact, they must remain secret; she made a solemn vow to herself—absolutely secret. A profound shiver rose along her spine to the nape of her neck. It's only fear, she said to herself. Everyone thought she was brave, and instead she was more afraid than the others. So afraid that she didn't even have the courage to confess it. Needles that suck blood, scissors that cut the skin, tubes in the throat. The torture chamber. She had glimpsed it twice and didn't want to see it again. She didn't even want to imagine it.

She returned to her armchair and covered herself well; then she turned on the television and tried to follow an old film that had just begun. She had a secret, she said over and over, and she did well to repeat it to herself. If she kept the secret to herself, she would be saved.

From time to time she looked at the violets, which from a suitable distance went back to resembling delicate violets; or she looked outside where it was growing dark. The sky was clear, still reddish above the roofs opposite. High up, the first big stars were shining. They announced another night of frost, a beautiful, silent night.

When the movie was finished, she prepared a light meal, some broth with rice and stracchino cheese. She gave up red wine and coffee without much effort, but not her after-dinner cigarette, which she smoked with enjoyment as she leafed through a magazine. At about eleven she again touched the glands under her arms and verified that they did not hurt. According to an article she had recently read, the absence of pain was always a good sign. Or did it say the opposite? She didn't remember. After the news she turned off the TV and lowered the light. The silence was perfect. Frost glittered on the rooftops; the sky was black and deep blue, limitless. A nocturnal bird, perhaps the only living thing in motion at that hour, flew from one roof to the next. Luisa stood at the window for a long time, her hands and legs warmed by the radiator, and her eyes fixed on the dark roofs of the houses. She thought of her father and mother who appeared silently inside her and now watched her without looking at her, with the inexpressive eyes they had in photographs.

They had nothing to say. Maybe they were always there, day and night, rain or shine. Her house attracted the dead like the wounded attract vultures. The dead felt neither cold nor heat; they were immaterial, perfect. But if they were perfect, what need did they have of her? Were they showing their affection this way? Burning out her light bulbs one after another? In just a few days three had stopped working: in the hall, in the storeroom, and in the little guest room. A strange phenomenon in which she could recognize the impetuosity of her father. As when he found her at trade union or political demonstrations where he took her unbeknownst to her mother. He discussed and argued, and soon lost her in the crowd, but he always found her again. Perhaps he let her wander away only a few meters, without losing sight of her. A few moments of fear, and she saw him coming, pushing aside the men with his elbows like dolls. He picked her up and put her on his shoulders for safety. Then she raised her arm and the world changed; she was the queen of Egypt, and the sea of heads swayed toward her. Her subjects. Who greeted her with the red banner of the empire, and she waved back her little flag in a ladylike way, responding to all so as not to offend her people.

Now, in order to catch her up again, her father was trying to appear with all his strength, but he only managed to burn out the light bulbs. He no longer had a body, poor man. The spirit had darted out of the body and wandered freely in space. Whether it was hot or cold. The spirits of her near ones did not frighten her. Also because she didn't really sense them. It was she who imagined them. It made her more afraid to imagine them absent, as they really were.

Strange violets, to look at them closely, very beautiful and nauseating, cloying, carriers of death. The disease had come at the same time they did. A strange coincidence. She thought of Laura as a demon. And when Laura called her one day to propose a visit, she treated her coldly, as she had Renata during the final days. I'm leaving, she said, sorry. The devil in person, that woman. She knew it from her cheerfulness, her health. From that blonde head of hair, still alive and young like a wild bush. Maybe she exaggerated, but the idea of making conversation nauseated her and increased her weakness. With that one, that old woman dressed like a young girl!

Luckily she discovered that there was a soccer match, she wasn't sure for which cup or championship. For some time she had liked to watch the soccer matches. She also kept up with a sports program. She was moved when they interviewed a defeated player at the end of the game: sweaty, dejected, tired with a mortal tiredness, his head hanging. Losing a soccer match isn't the end of the world, boys! That was her advice, but she understood their bad mood. Young men don't know how to lose; they can't deal with it. She drifted from following the game and began to think of Bruno. She stopped seeing the two teams struggling after the ball; she found herself with Bruno again as if she were really seeing him, as if her house were a boat with Bruno silently at the oars. He was an excellent rower. He had a two or three days' beard; the muscles of his shoulders were tight and round. The soft sound of the water, which she also liked. In the bottom of the boat two fingers of warm, grayish water and a fishing rod that rolled back and forth with an odd sound. It was the reel that struck against wood at every thrust of the oars. "Five barbels," Bruno said with satisfaction. And he added with a snigger, "Big fisherman of barbels." He had been tender talking like that. When they were out in a boat, all was well. Only barbels, poor dear, never a trout.

She rose with a smile on her lips and went to get an olive. She chose a big, green emerald and found it delicious. For weeks she had been eating only cookies, rice in broth, and olives. When she was troubled by stomach acidity, she ate three or four olives, the large, green ones that lasted longer than barley candies. On that day she had eaten six of them. Wild fennel, water and salt, the silvery film that forms on water. She liked to drink cold water after having eaten an olive. What an extraordinary sensation of coolness, of aromas multiplied by water. There were only a few olives remaining in the bottom of the jar; by now there was not much of anything in the fridge. The thought of going out seemed absurd to her, and she decided that tomorrow she would phone the grocer. She hadn't ever done that, but for once she might avail herself.

Fortunately, there are olives in the world, and comfortable armchairs, television programs made to pass the time, as well as films and mystery stories, grocers who bring your purchases home for you, canaries that sing. In the other apartments they were preparing dinner, they opened and closed faucets, many flushed their toilets, they watched television news, or animated cartoons, or pay-per-view broadcasts. The man on the floor above, an athletic young fellow, urinated vigorously, so much so that Luisa raised her eyes to the ceiling. A long, loud splash of water right over her head, to which the canary answered with the sweetest of songs. If her neighbors lived normally, she did not hate them; on the contrary, they kept her company; she didn't get angry if every now and then something fell to the floor. She, too, understood that lids easily fall down, and after the clatter they begin to roll threateningly, foretelling more clatter. These were peaceful domestic sounds. The cars hurrying homeward were also nothing but simple means of transportation with their heaters turned up high. Holy winter, Luisa thought, blessed are the frozen cities that will always be filled with peace.

After the soccer, a program of entertainment began, conducted by two very elegant hosts, a man and a woman, well mannered, cultivated, but also simple and funny. One was hardly aware that they were performing. The man in particular had the air of a big, intelligent, well-brought-up boy, and from time to time he sat down at the piano and sang an old song. On their program there appeared actors, politicians, and international celebrities from Africa, Australia, America. The hosts asked intelligent questions and seemed old friends of everyone. How the devil did they manage to know so many people, so many films, and books, and concerts. . . . Luisa was ready to acknowledge the superiority of others when it was so obvious. The two hosts surely earned excellent salaries, many millions of lire a day, but how many qualities they had. And how much knowledge and self-confidence and attractiveness. She tried to imagine them in their private lives but couldn't. She was barely able to picture a grand room, its floor of expensive wood strewn with pastel-colored rugs, and two long, leather divans. Nothing else.

Halfway through the program her nausea came back. At those moments she smelled a disagreeable odor like that of burnt flesh. She always ran to the bathroom even if she knew that she would not vomit. She rinsed her mouth and cooled her forehead. Then she fixed her hair and went back to the living room. She knew very well that she was alone there too, but the two hosts were a sort of deputation from the human race, and so certain things had to be done in the bathroom, like cutting one's nails or squeezing blackheads.

She wrapped herself in a blanket and went back to watching the broadcast. She felt sick and well at the same time. The sensations were intermingled. In the space of a minute she could pass back and forth three times from the gloomiest unhappiness to the brightest joy. She thought a great deal about the stupendous month of January, icy and sunny, generous in its sunsets and dawns, and its wind even beautiful. Beautiful, ugly. Good, bad. In their continual alternation she began to doubt their reality. The house, on the other hand, always belonged to her; the armchair was comfortable, the television turned on. She never forgot the enormous privilege of her circumstances that allowed her to shut herself up in a well-heated house during the coldest month of the year. In fact, she felt a strange uneasiness, a mute sense of guilt; she feared being singled out and condemned by others. As usual, she fell asleep late in front of the television; then she went to the bedroom, chilled and with eyes half closed in order not to wake up completely. Thinking only that sleep was the most beautiful thing in the world. This evening she left the light on in the kitchen, and in the morning she couldn't see it. She kept being surprised at the short life of her bulbs, but she left them on day and night. When it was nine o'clock, she phoned the grocer and asked the shop boy to buy her some bulbs and a carton of cigarettes. Her shopping list was so long that she could ask for the favor without having to pay. The boy promised that he would come round at ten, and she concerned herself with making a bit of order. She was weak but without particular complaints and in a very good mood, only a little slow in her movements, a little cloudy from sleep that did not quite satisfy her. Even if she slept ten hours a day in two or three installments, it was never enough. Her body defended itself from its ailments with sleep. At ten, punctually,

blurred images on the screen were actually showing a breath-taking moment of the climb: the sky around the climber and above the spur of rock from which he hung was a stupendous blue.

But her cousin didn't care for the mountains. She poured out her how are you, are you getting around, the doctor, shopping, why a shop boy when I'm here, and so on and so forth.

"I don't need anything, thanks," Luisa said, raising her voice a little. She hated this insistence. Then she became aware of going too far and admitted to feeling irritable. She said good-bye trying to sound affectionate, and her voice came out squeaky. Her mother, too, used to overdo gratitude. She thanked tradesmen, brush salesmen, the little man who came to read the meter. Luisa remembered well the sweet smile that always accompanied her thanks, and always seemed wasted to her, given away to unknowns who didn't deserve it. Some men might have deceived themselves about that smile. Her mother's mouth was neither too big nor too small; it was perfect. It began with two deep dimples, and from the dimples came two fine lines that framed it. The smile was inside; even when her mother was upset or not talking to anyone or washing the dishes, her lips were slightly drawn up and it seemed that she was smiling. When she said "thanks," the lips parted and showed her compact teeth, which had become irregular only in the last months of her illness. At the end the smile was disfigured, but the lips remained beautiful. Even in death her mother's face was beautiful and serene. She shouldn't remember her only with that face of a corpse. The weeks and months of her long martyrdom. She was able, if she wanted, not to think of them, but those weeks, moment by moment, were always inside her and would die only with her. The arms ruined by needles for feeding and medicine. The skin hanging from the arms. The cuts, marks of the needles. The sores. It was nothing but three days on the cross. She bore witness to it without malice, out of simple truth. Her mother had died like Jesus, her father had died like Jesus, without lungs and with heart decayed. Long crucifixions. Both had remained good-looking even when dead. She remembered them more handsome than their companions in death. The old woman with her swollen belly and cheap rosary, her face already a skull that had belonged for years to the kingdom of the dead. The old man made of wax, as small as a baby. The young woman mourned by her husband and even by the nurses who had taken care of her for days. The morphine, the chief doctor who didn't want to give her mother morphine so that she wouldn't become addicted. The Catholic chief doctor. She wished him for the thousandth time to feel the same pains her mother had felt. Nevertheless, her mother's smile was so beautiful, everyone envied her that smile, everyone became more kind with her. Luisa closed her blissful eyes and imagined those lips coming close to her, to her forehead, and kissing her with such delicacy that she shivered; and then two little tears escaped her.

It could be any time of the day. Six in the evening, but also eleven, or maybe three. But they had rung at the door below, and continued to ring insistently. She gave in with distaste and went to answer. It was her cousin, who was now disturbing her for the second time in one day. She looked at herself and saw that her robe was open and her pajamas were all rumpled. She barely had time to fix herself a little before her cousin appeared, bursting with health.

"Did you think I would give up so easily?" she bragged.

"What a surprise," Luisa whispered. But she couldn't bring herself to tell her she was pleased.

The cousin came in and took off her gloves and sheepskin coat and then a scarf and sweater of blue wool.

"With this weather, how do you manage to keep from getting sick?" she said, sitting down on the new couch.

"In fact, here I am."

Luisa seated herself in an armchair and tried to comb her hair as best she could with her hands.

"I must not look very good," she said, trying to smile.

"No. As far as that goes, you don't look good. Luisetta, you've got to take care of yourself, we're not little girls anymore."

"But not old wrecks yet," she answered.

"If I don't tell you, no one else will," the cousin went on. "You look bad, I sensed it. You have the shop boy bring your groceries as if you've got no one. Tomorrow I'll bring you some things early."

"I have everything already."

"And if you were less unreasonable, I could also say to you: Pack your suitcase, dress warmly, and come with me. There's an empty bedroom that we never use. And a bathroom too."

Luisa thought for a few seconds and began to laugh. "But for goodness' sake," she let slip. And said no more because she did not want to offend her cousin. She might have said: I don't know what time it is; I don't even know the day; I can't remember if I've had supper, but I wouldn't come with you if I were at death's door. I would rather call a doctor. But she thought this only as a measure of absurdity. However, her cousin took note of the laugh and remained silent for a long time. Perhaps she was thinking: If she's as rude as she usually is, it means she's not in such a bad way.

"What were you watching?" she asked, turning her preoccupied gaze to the television set which was still on.

"Nothing special." It was a program about the stock exchange. Boring and incomprehensible, so she couldn't pretend to have been interested in it.

"I think you're run down," the cousin said. "And just re-tiring like that, it's not a game."

"The doctor said I was in good shape," Luisa lied. "Signs of age, osteoporosis . . . but everything else is all right." Actually she thought her cousin was right. She was worn out. She had heard it much talked about, and now it was her turn. A serious state of exhaustion.

She changed channels and stopped at a musical program, which luckily distracted her cousin. She, on the other hand, felt a longing for an olive. She went into the kitchen and put a few olives in a dish.

"Try one," she said to her cousin, "they're delicious." She wanted to be rid of her and offered her the beloved olives. The cousin devoured four or five without saying a word and dropped two pits outside of the ashtray. She chewed thought-fully like a cow; after all, such had been her upbringing. By now she had improved herself somewhat, but there was no clothing that could hide the crudeness. Five olives, while Luisa still had the first in her mouth almost whole.

"Did you park nearby?" she asked.

"In front of the entrance. There's no one around this evening. All those awful boys in the bar must be a misery."

"I know, I know." It seemed too private a subject to dis-cuss with her cousin.

"You find syringes?"

"No, no syringes. But they're disgusting all the same."

"Too bad, because it's really nice around here. The center is still the center: the roofs, the towers. We see four little Christmas trees and a few balconies. There's the supermarket downstairs, that yes, it's a piece of good luck. I can go down without a coat, even for just a loaf of bread."

"What time has it gotten to be?" Luisa asked.

"Nine-thirty. Are you going to bed?"

years when she was healthy, when the mouth tasted and the stomach did its work in perfect accord with the rest of the body. She remembered running and swimming and dozens of happy days that by now she alone could remember. And her doctor came back to mind. She thought that maybe he could have helped her. But if on the other hand he hadn't been able to do anything for her, wouldn't she be feeling even worse than she felt? Wouldn't the doctors have tortured her uselessly as they had her mother? When one is alone, one can deceive oneself easily if one wants to. There's nothing wrong with you, you're just exhausted, it will pass. It did her good to tell herself so. In this way sleep returned to her.

In the days and weeks that followed she learned to struggle against panic. Panic always welled up unexpectedly, first in the center of her chest, but after a few minutes her brain was dazed and produced strange thoughts. They're all alive and don't give a damn about me. And who knows how long they'll live. They drive cars, plan vacations, and if they imagine a seriously ill woman, they pity her from the heart, saying "That's life," and then they think no more about it. But after all, what the devil are they supposed to do; they can't be accused of anything. She envied their health with an intensity never felt before, sometimes ferociously. They went around, those out there, with the good fresh air in their lungs. While she was alone, battling against fear, which at a certain point went out of her and into the objects surrounding her. The ashtray became strange. The pen next to the telephone made her cry. Her red lighter disgusted her. Her body was alien, her house, the city itself. She shouldn't try to stifle the panic. She ought to let it escape. She ought to think of the grave, of putrefaction, of nothingness. If she felt like crying, she cried as long as she could. Finally the panic died down, and worn out and with a headache, she could say to herself: It will go away, it's exhaustion, it will go away. Then she added something to the shopping list that she would read over the phone, or she read a couple of pages of a mystery and fell asleep in front of the TV.

11

WATER AND SUGAR, OLIVES, A LITTLE TEA, VERY
sweet, with lemon. She couldn't get down anything
else. The days lengthened; the temperature rose. It
was spring. The mole on her collarbone was no
longer a mole. Now she knew it. She had become
adept at changing the dressing in the bath without
turning on the light, but she had touched it. The
glands had not changed at all, and she had almost
become used to them. Maybe she had had them for
a long time and just had never noticed them. The
mole, on the other hand, had gotten much larger. It
wasn't a mole.

One night she screwed up her courage and
looked at it, partly because it could no longer be
hidden by two large plasters. It looked like the
black droppings of a wild animal. Dry and black, it
also resembled lava. She touched it with the tip of
her finger and it was not sensitive to touch. It did
not repel her too much. But as she looked at it, she
became aware that it gave off a nasty smell, and she

became frightened; she sprayed a little perfume and decided to call a doctor, or an ambulance, the police, her cousin, Walter, Renata—everyone in other words. Only thus, making a list of names and having the telephone within reach of her hand, did she succeed in calming herself. They would be here in an instant; they wouldn't leave me alone. Another minute and I'll call. She hadn't recognized for a long time her real enemy; she was a stupid, foolish woman! Suddenly the armchair seemed uncomfortable, and she went to stretch out on the couch, holding the telephone to her chest and caressing it like a precious thing. On the couch the air from the air conditioner came like a clean, light wind; she almost seemed to be in the country. Swallows flew and made their shrill cries. She concentrated on her breath, imagining the long and inaccessible route it must follow, a cave of dark flesh without a glimmer of light, up, up as far as the lips; and then other fresh air sent to the lungs, what an effort, the same long route, up and down, in and out, a breath of wind a few centimeters long, like a cigarette, like a little animal that doesn't know where to go, whether up or down in that dark cave of flesh. How hard it was to stay alive; how tirelessly the body worked. And she had never given it any respect, never paid any attention to it.

No doctors, she said to herself proudly. A body this expert can't be killed so easily. She must leave it alone, protect its secret absolutely, keep it away from the dangerous influences of others. If you say that you're sick, then you're done for; just saying it to yourself will kill you. Everybody tries to get in where there's a little happiness, and if they can't take away what you have, they'll try to dirty it for you. It's the same way viruses and sicknesses get inside you because you're their food; they take advantage of your weakness and eat you alive. Disgusting young men, viruses, mosquitoes, lazy, helpless people, ugly little plastic puppets: there's nothing else on the face of the earth! Why stay, then? Oh, if she had had a daughter she would have fought. Think of the courage a mother must have, the most desperate courage, that while you're dying it makes you clench your fists and pray and even curse because it's impossible to accept the idea you're leaving a child behind. Yes, even curse. A curse, too, can reach the ears of God like a prayer. She'd done her part, now it was God's turn to do his. If he existed. If he didn't exist, a person without children like her could say to hell with it all.

There was something comical even in pain. Which now was radiating out slightly from her spine, and especially from her kidneys, to her legs. She tried to understand what exactly pain consisted of. It's the same stuff as thoughts, not like fire or like ice. Pain itself, if it goes too far, doesn't take itself seriously. The bad smell coming from the two plasters, yes, that is a problem. The perfume she had sprayed only partly covered it.

She did not call anyone. She collected all the perfumes she had in the house and tried them one after another. She found that one she had considered too ladylike and never cared for was best adapted against the smell and decided to keep it always within reach.

If she was not restless, the hours flew by, the days and nights flew by. Her ever-shorter shopping list and the weekly telephone call to the grocer were her only duties. The shop boy asked no questions; he had gotten used to the tip and her state of illness, and he willingly took care of a few small chores for her. She liked to see him. She thought him rather cute and droll; he must have been dissatisfied with his side-burns, he was always changing their shape. One day she thought it would be nice to give him a kiss, and laughing at herself, she almost apologized for having the thought. Actually, she had no desire to be kissed. She only was trying to distract herself. She didn't even keep track of the passing days. The sky and the clouds, the moon, the stars said nothing in particular to her. A glass and a star were all the same.

She eagerly followed the soccer matches and luckily several were broadcast during this period. The extraordinary efforts of the players, those powerful calves, those jumps, kicks, and falls, their ability to get back on their feet. She never tired of admiring them, as if they were all her sons who filled her with pride. Tall and strong. Maybe her father would have liked a son, tall and strong; Bruno, too, would have liked one.

Beside the swallows many other birds flew around the house: sparrows, certainly, and perhaps doves. Her canary tried to converse with all of them, imitating even the simple call of the sparrow. Luisa had never listened attentively to the song of the wild birds. She discovered it one afternoon. Below in the street, car horns and shouts of the young men; up above, the birds indifferent to noise, absorbed in their melodious outpouring of sounds. The particular calls could signify nothing, that was why she had never noticed them; but altogether they formed an undulating music that must have a precise meaning. Not even the raucous passing of a blackbird, who cried from one window and then another, was able to interrupt the celebration. The birds ignored him, singing only among themselves, and if one paid close attention, one could distinguish an impertinent voice, the whistle of a tough kid, a monotone, a bass. Singers at their level should have found the noises of the street unbearable, but instead they sang.

She singled out one with a small voice like that of a cricket, but who in the space of a second poured out very softly at least ten notes, and she imagined it to be tiny, with a pointed beak, all eyes and feathers. Hardly anything, even in comparison with her canary. The skin under the feathers must be almost transparent, and its little heart must pulse inside like a miracle. She imagined this minuscule heart resting on the tip of her index finger, and staring at her raised finger, she was deeply moved.

Once she also heard the graceless call of ducks, who must have risen in flight from the lake in the park. They did this rarely and only toward sunset. Maybe they were duck weddings, flying processions.

She never answered the telephone, which rang from time to time. She had told Renata and her cousin that she was going to leave for the baths.

When the phone rang, Laura came to mind. She imagined a story. Laura was moved by her condition and helped her day and night; she prepared unusual herb teas that cured her. She woke up one morning and realized that she was completely well. I'm cured! she said to the people she met in her fantasy: the grocer's boy, the vegetable man, the policemen, Renata perhaps, her cousin. . . .

She dreamed more than once of being cured, but it was a false dream that was bad for her. She was not being cured and not getting better; on the contrary, she was getting worse. She felt weaker all the time and more fragile. She walked as little as possible and very slowly, because of the pain in her legs and her absurd fear of breaking something, of falling to the ground with all her bones broken. Her bones felt like glass; she must be careful not to break them, extremely careful. Thus she went to the bathroom sliding along in her slippers and supporting herself against the walls of the hallway.

When the tenants on the floor above returned from a trip, their balcony was filled with enormous skindivers' suits put out to dry, and the sparrows changed balconies. The monsters are back, Luisa said to herself disconsolately. The suits swayed slightly in a breath of wind, and she, who could see them barely a few centimeters away, became aware that they were very exotic objects: where had they been, these suits. . . . The ocean, the big fish of the documentaries, the coral reefs, the jellyfish. . . . What a couple, those two on the top floor; they seemed stupid, but in fact they ventured out into the oceans.

Until then none of the tenants had taken note of her condition. She heard them when they went out and when they came in, when they walked around and talked loud, when they urinated, or set the table or turned on the TV. The young men at the bar had also increased out of all proportion. A mob of shouting people until three in the morning. Instead of getting upset then and there as she had at the arrival of the couple upstairs, she began a new phase that very much surprised her.

She discovered that her body had adapted to its new situation, and she began to manage fairly well. She could walk almost normally, slowly but without dragging her feet. She could even eat spaghetti with butter and plenty of Parmesan cheese on it. If she didn't try to hurry, she could also operate the vacuum cleaner and wipe up in the kitchen. While cleaning the birdcage, she ascertained that the canary had no intention of escaping and did not take advantage of the slowness of her movements. The bottom of the cage was open, and he swung peacefully, pecking at his feathers. That was when she decided to leave the door of the cage open all the time. By now he was grown up, and he wouldn't hurt himself flying into the walls. He was a sensible and polite little bird. The most delicate and gentle creature in the world. Luisa was afraid of forgetting his food and letting him die of hunger. On certain days after the terrible discovery of the growth, she had only remembered to take away his cloth after noon. She must foresee every danger, think about everything now when she was lucid. At certain moments she felt so confused.

During the warmest hours she stretched out on the couch, which she had covered with a fine linen sheet, and dreamed with open eyes or watched TV. If the canary made a timid sortie from his cage, she enjoyed watching him. He jumped for long distances on the carpet and looked around, sometimes supporting himself elegantly on only one leg. He especially looked at her, lying on the couch; she smiled at him and whistled a call. Then he suddenly flew up on the wardrobe and from there went back to his cage to eat. He slept and sang only in the cage.

In order to avoid continually seeing the ugly growth, one afternoon Luisa put an old linen towel around her neck, its ends tucked under the elastic of her pajamas. When she looked at herself in the big bedroom mirror, she laughed because she thought she resembled a pianist she often saw on TV, with eyeglasses like hers and a silk scarf under her evening blouse. All white in her large pajamas, her face tired and thin as it had not been for years, her glasses lit by a ray of sunshine filtered through the shutters, she might also have looked like a mad sister.

They were yelling in the street, motorcycles passed by, the birds sang on the roofs, a television gentleman commented with disproportionate passion on a tennis match. A young sparrow rested on the kitchen windowsill and looked at her without fear. He had bright feathers and a proud air, the bright eyes of youth. All the beings surrounding her had more life than she.

The sun turned orange and illuminated the knickknacks and the rug, gilding them. A ray fell upon the crystal chandelier making a brilliant display of light that enchanted her; the entire rainbow was spread in a long curve on the white rug. Then she saw her father. Perhaps she imagined it, perhaps she dreamed it, but without moving a millimeter from her couch, not even in the dream. Her father in flesh and bone, seated before her. Dressed in his best clothes, his mustache clipped, his face serious. They looked at one another for a few seconds, then Luisa's eyes turned down because she wanted to see all of him, and she noticed that her father's appearance was ancient. The shoes were very new, but of a model never seen. Slightly dusty. And where the heels rested on the carpet they did not press it down.

The sparrow had come back to stare at her and challenged her with its call. And the kitchen was gilded by the sun, and the marble, and the pots, as well as the impertinent sparrow, who ought to have made friends with the canary. Her father seemed to have disappeared, but if she closed her eyes she sensed him still there, wrapped in the odor of old cloth. She remembered when he had said laughing, "I forgive you, and if you don't want to be forgiven, I forgive you just the same." He was coming from the inn and was a little tipsy. The heavy material of his jacket. She opened her eyes and looked at the sparrow again, who now turned its back and sang to the street. She saw it very clearly even though it was at least five meters away. She reached instinctively for her glasses and realized that she didn't have them. In fact, they were on the carpet next to a magazine. She opened her eyes wide and turned to look at the sparrow. She saw it without her glasses or rather saw it better than she remembered ever having seen it, even as a little girl.

She could see the television perfectly also. How many incredible things were happening in her body. She got up very slowly and went to the window giggling like a little girl. What she saw was an extraordinary miracle: the dark blue of the sky, the limpid blue lower down, interrupted by the black profile of the roofs, the warm yellow that lit up the kitchen, a child in the house opposite watching TV, the red tablecloth already laid out in the dining room, and the couches, the photographs hung on the walls. The lights that ran around the canopy of the building were simple glass boxes containing three neon tubes and not the great fiery rows she had seen for years. She hadn't thought that things were so well separated from one another. The young men, the lights of their motorbikes, the license plates, the sign of the bar: everything perfectly ablaze.

She went back to lie down on the couch and spent several minutes contemplating details of the house: the weave of the curtains, the sharp outlines of the television screen. . . . She was unable to raise her spirits with her reborn power of sight because she knew it was bound up with the disease that had invaded her, and the disease was there under the linen towel and it persecuted her with its foul odor, like the black vortex of the old films when they plunged into the past or in the maw of a dead star, or on the roller coaster when you lose your breath. She remained with her eyes closed for a long time to protect herself from despair, and she fell asleep. She hadn't turned off the air conditioner, and the cool air entered into her dreams, unfortunately bringing with it an ugly demon in the form of a pig. A pig wider than it was long, with a huge mouth, and claws as well. He wanted something in particular, and she stupidly had forgotten it: the little girl in the cradle! She had a child and was unable to protect it. In the demon's mouth! who is now jumping in the road even though there was no road in Luisa's house, and he begins to climb like a trapeze artist with his food in his mouth. Luisa squeezes into the chimney flue and tries to climb up, and the road is really her tomb, and the child is Luisa herself, and the devil was no one but death, who wanted only her.

She woke but did not feel upset. She had been afraid and her body had not moved. It had not reacted. Only this useless gift of sight, which at bottom did her harm because the house looked less nice to her than it did before, full of defects. The stars, too, were less interesting, simple pinheads in the sky. They were showing a good play on television that she had already seen. That was just what she wanted. She

154

could follow it now and then without losing the thread. The sound track was very beautiful, soft and danceable. A little later, at a perfect moment of the film, when he and she were kissing under a tree, she said to herself softly: It's the end, Luì, maybe the end has come. She felt more excited than frightened. Excited like a schoolgirl on her first trip. Overcome by a sudden tenderness toward herself, she imagined that it would be good to play the piano before dying, play it for herself. But she contented herself with the rich sound track of the film. The minutes she spent immersed in a film were precious, because she did not think and was not assailed by attacks of panic. All she had to do was avoid sudden movements; sometimes it took only a movement of her hand and all her pains were reawakened and began to throb.

Tonight she did not even go to sleep in her bed. The old sheet of coarse linen that covered the couch kept its freshness better than the normal sheets, and besides, the air conditioner was in the living room as well as the TV, her preferred companion who didn't require her to make conversation. Blessed be he who had invented it. She regretted not lighting the blue lamp in the room more often, the most elegant thing in the whole house. She was too tired.

She didn't have to be ashamed of anything. She wasn't ashamed of anything in particular, but she was a little ashamed and did not know why. Her life was transparent. If she felt bad, she could pray. Good Lord Jesus, I look to you as a modest retiree, full of pains and stinking sores. Pity me, pity me. Even if I don't believe in you and your holy kingdom, have pity on me. Lord pity, Christ pity. As if entrusting herself to someone, her eyes closed and she grew peaceful. She slept without dreaming and woke when the sun rose and the swallows were chasing one another among the rooftops. The canary sang in its cage. She slept again for a long time and dreamlessly, and when she awoke the sky was blue and full of cheerful swallows. She was still able to see them very well. On the television they were replaying the talk show of the previous evening. She hadn't turned it off before falling asleep, and all the lights of the living room had remained on. It was an interesting program, and she followed it with attention.

Halfway through the morning the telephone began to ring, and it rang for a long time. A little later there was also repeated ringing at the door. It could only be her cousin. Perhaps she should telephone her again, to keep her from coming for a few weeks. Around dinner time she called and pretended to be cheerful.

"What do you mean, where am I? I'm at the baths. I'm well, of course I'm well. I don't know when I'll be back."

Her cousin's advice was as usual: keep warm and don't tire yourself, but before hanging up she said, "You don't know how much I would like to know what you're plotting, because you must be plotting something."

Luisa laughed and allowed the promise of more telephone calls to be extracted. Then she invented an excuse to put down the receiver before the cousin could ask her for the number at the baths "in case of any eventuality."

Luì is like the elephants: she imagined this phrase and put it in the ugly but dear mouth of Renata. Even if she wasn't an eagle, she had her kind sensitivity and tender heart. Who knows if her children will ever accomplish anything worthwhile, or if they're already lost like the ones at the bar. Poor Renata, she'll have a load of troubles from them and few satisfactions.

For several minutes she had been hearing a song different from the usual one. They were turtledoves! Undoubtedly, they were turtledoves! She would have loved to be able to see them, but she did not feel strong enough to get up. Lord, I beg you, let me see them now, let me be able to see them, let me have a good look at them. It was given to her to see them, if only in flight as they crossed her field of vision heading toward the park. They were two young turtledoves flying elegantly, flying as if they must have a clear idea of the place where they would meet, perhaps on a beautiful, high branch, or on the roof of the ice-cream stand where some child would wonder at them.

For many hours she had no other pleasures. It was a damp day, a day that made her legs suffer. She wept a little, almost with an effort, and whispered through her sobs that she did not want to die. The usual trick to make herself fall asleep. In fact, she drowsed off, but each time she opened her eyes and contemplated a little crack in the ceiling, or one of Laura's violets, or she listened to the canary's song, or the call of the turtledoves. As the hours passed the towel around her neck became oppressive. She freed herself from it, swearing that she wouldn't look at herself.

In the afternoon—the sky had grown cloudy and there was a smell of rain—she went to the bathroom and was forced to do things she would never have wanted to do, but she had gotten to the bottom of a problem, and when she came back to the couch, she thanked the Lord, the only spirit who did not feel disgust for her.

Her husband. She smiled. Her husband who doesn't exist, pure as a turtledove.

By now, day and night were becoming confused. She opened her eyes and didn't even ask herself if it was day or night. As long as this state of profound torpor lasted, she felt blessed like a child. Even her pains seemed far away. Her body was finally resting. She felt lighter, almost well. In reality her body was icy. The air conditioner was too close, just a meter from her feet.

The particularly loud roar of a motor shook her, but she was not able to recognize it. She thought it was thunder moving across the sky. She imagined it as it fell into a long tunnel of clouds.

She was behind an angel in flight.

Luisa rises to the sky in her father's arms.

Her father had been a member of the Socialist Party, but he became a solitary who no longer believes in anything. He lives there and wears beautiful holiday shoes and a suit of old-fashioned cut.

She had already seen him once and knows he's there.

But no one is there.

Clouds like a field of grain. Absolute nothing. Wind of the heavens. *Wooo. . . .*

There are no other beings. There's the void. Only an ancient wind, born God knows where.

Something completely different.

They were broadcasting an endless tennis match on television; the smack-smack kept her company along with the solicitous voice of the commentator, who seemed a decent devil. He didn't want to disturb the players by talking too loud and whispered as if he were in church.

When Luisa began to come back to herself, displeased and disappointed because she had been very happy, she was welcomed by the voice that had kept her company for so many hours together with the smack-smack of the tennis balls, and she thought she had slept for the length of a match. In reality, the tournament had gone on for three days.

What a stupid thing it was to wake up. The pains lay in wait under her skin, waking more slowly than she. The smells, on the other hand, assailed her immediately. Especially the sour smell of urine that must have been coming up from the street. The thought came to her of her old doll, and she was enraged: it should have been at the end of the couch or on the armchair, someplace easy to see, but it wasn't. Her cousin must have stolen it; she had been a thief even when she was a girl, and in fact once they had pinched something in a perfume store. She cursed her and hated her with all the strength remaining to her. And she'll steal money too; the old whore is waiting for nothing else. She knew her only too well. One of those who when she was a girl took it from behind so she could remain a virgin. And the daughter must be the same. Of course she liked the city center; she would be at her ease among the mob of pests and thieves exactly like herself. It did her good, at least for a little while, to get angry. Her color came back and her body began to warm up again. The pains then weren't so unbearable. She couldn't feel at all a spot on her hip that had caused her great agony, and she almost missed it, because at that spot the pain contained a tiny physical pleasure that she couldn't exactly remember now. A slight sting like that hidden in the flesh of the fingertips, which can be felt when the fingers are pushed against a wall or the corners of doors. She sat up, and then very slowly got to her feet using the back of a chair as a support. Moving from one chair to another, she could reach either the kitchen or the bathroom with little effort. Before going into the bathroom, she remembered that she didn't have the towel around her throat, and she carefully avoided looking at herself in the mirror. She did see something even without turning around, more a sensation than an actual sight. A dark stain at the base of her throat. Her pajamas were dirty and weren't easy to take off. Then she got under the shower and stood motionless for a long time. She had to be very careful. Move slowly, pick up the soap gently, wash with care especially the intimate parts. Paying close attention so as not to lose her balance, she scrubbed her head well. Then she turned off the shower and began to dry herself. She dropped the wet towel to the floor and walked on it so as not to slip.

She also tried to clean her teeth but immediately had to spit out the toothpaste, which had a nauseating taste and made her stomach turn.

She hid the stain with a light cotton towel that resembled a scarf and put on larger pajamas than the others. On the floor several things had piled up that needed to be washed. She sat on the bed and helplessly contemplated the heap of laundry, which the blue lamp made to resemble a glacier or a crèche with all of the grotto.

Below in the street a young man sang at the top of his lungs in order to tease someone, and others shouted and laughed. They were like a pack of dogs. On the floor above, on the other hand, there were strangers. Someone who spoke in a deep voice, and a woman with a foreign accent who giggled sensuously. Then the deep voice became alarmed and began to shout. When the shots rang out and the usual chase began with a loud siren, Luisa understood that she was overhearing a television film. From the footsteps it seemed to her that the woman must be at home alone. There, now she's going out on the terrace. Now she's changing the program because the film is over. Now she's going to the bathroom just overhead, and she's washing her hands for a long time.

In front of the garage the game of kicking a ball against the wall started up again, and naturally they began to yell once more. A big motorcycle started off at full throttle. She remembered the old man who had shot at a youth and blessed him tenderly. Maybe he was still languishing in a wretched cell, or maybe he had hanged himself in protest, to the great satisfaction of those who still wept crocodile tears over the poor, maladjusted young man. Their democratic officials! The reactionaries were scoundrels, but these were sly and false. Didn't her father also say that?

Here and there in the neighborhood the various themes of news programs followed one another. Everybody's windows were open, all no doubt in their underwear in front of the television, hoping for a thunderstorm that would bring the summer to an end. Poor deluded souls; tomorrow ends and the day after tomorrow begins. She was no longer adapted to live this life; she was good only for sleeping. There always seemed more of the young men; she could still hear the noise they made walking all together from one sidewalk to the other. She thought of throwing her nails; she even thought of throwing herself, but she didn't like that. It seemed too humiliating. Half naked, crushed in the middle of the street. She shivered just thinking of it. Shivers and sweat, surely caused by a too hot shower. What a rotten season, summer. You wash and you're already sweating.

Lord, she whispered, I used to feel so good. Let me sleep in peace, amen. Because I'm really tired of it all. I appreciated many things, sunsets spaghetti with clams the blue lamp you see lit near me and also my car and Renata and naturally my parents, but now I'm so sick and only sleep does me good, and I'm alone and we don't have to involve anyone else in this matter. Thank you for not having me found even by that thief, my cousin. I go willingly; I don't give a damn for all the nice things I'm leaving behind. But if she took the doll, I beg you to throw her into the inferno of thieves. And if instead Bruno took it, even if I don't believe that, pardon him because he's only a poor fool and you know it.

The bedroom, without the air conditioner, was decidedly too warm; besides, the couch was new and it bothered her to have used it so little. And the blue lamp, she thought, if I don't look at it for at least five minutes a day, what the devil did I buy it for! Slowly she came back to the chairs and took the path to the kitchen. She drank a cup of tea and ate two or three olives. Of course, her digestive system couldn't function well on a diet like that, but she was not hungry; maybe the bottom of her stomach was completely wasted away and the food fell directly into the intestines. Lord, how can a woman live without a stomach? And she thought that maybe her prayers were not being heard because of a problem of form. Even if she didn't know the words of the ritual, she decided she must show herself to be docile. She took the oil cruet and spilled a drop of olive oil on her index finger; then she made the sign of the cross on her forehead and her mouth, and although she didn't know the formula, she said out loud: This is the holy oil of the Lord. She said it just a few centimeters from the canary, who was out of its cage and stared at her huddled on the dish rack. The oil had an extraordinary perfume; it smelled of hills and tree bark, and besides it was warm, not the disgusting warmth of water or tea at room temperature but a noble warmth, a warmth that was spreading on her forehead and would help her to slip away from the body without suffering, like a newborn emerging from a mother of many children.

She filled a plastic bottle with water and carried it to the living room as a reserve for the night. The youths in the street were laughing now, many with a shrill, falsetto sound. *Uuuu, Iiiii, Uuuu.* . . . She had to forget about them, think only of her poor legs, stiff and painful, of the bottle that slipped in her fingers, of her grip on the chairs that shook and threatened to abandon her; she must be careful, but the noise of the youths soiled even her prayers and made them sound ridiculous. She could not ignore them at all. Not even a hair of your head will be forgotten. But it's not possible that young men like these deserve to be remembered, and for what then? Like me, after all, who's no good for anything anymore. She glimpsed for an instant the nurse who was chewing American gum as she pressed her index finger on her mother's jugular and thought that no one would push her finger on her veins. What a privilege, what good luck.

She lay down on the couch sighing with relief, also because it was very cool and comfortable. Her bones needed a few minutes to adapt themselves to the new arrangement; they seemed to have lost their curved edges; they felt pointed and sharp against her flesh and conveyed to her the unmistakable order not to move. The holy oil did not get to them; they were only, after all, her carcass. She felt she was a spirit separated from the body. Submerged in the sky and in the flights of swallows, who now were preparing to leave for Africa. That was what the miracle of the eyes was for: to watch their perfect flights. Maybe it was the last time she was seeing them; she thought that this too had meaning.

She still felt a little anger about the stolen doll, her cousin's crudeness, and the crudeness in general of all women who have children on whose behalf they feel entitled to any dirty trick. Then she corrected herself: not all, perhaps her mother was not like that. She was not crude with anyone. She was always courteous. Strange that she didn't make herself seen. Only her father, with his wool suit and new shoes. Actually, she didn't see him but sensed him just outside her field of vision, exactly in front of the bathroom door. Her brave knight. The last man in the city. You hear them, Papa, screaming like pigs. They have no pity. Our neighborhood is worse than death.

The pain became so acute that it seemed not to have a particular point of origin in her body. Her whole body was pain. She wanted to tear it away with her hands but only managed to throw off the towel and pull away her pajamas. Without being aware of it, she uttered a continuous lament for hours, high pitched but weak, but none of the neighbors heard anything. She scratched the skin around the growth deeply and lost much blood. She didn't even notice that the canary, now almost without food, had decided to fly to the roof of the house opposite.

When she was able to calm herself, she fell into a deep

contemplation of the blue and white sky and heard once more the song of the birds. She was very weak, but serene too. Despite the smell of urine and sewage rising from the street. Her mind went back to an old joke she had told Bruno. The red tomatoes march in a row in the field; I am a tomato; I am a tomato. A turd follows them well pleased. . . . I am a tomato, I am a tomato. And the last tomato in the row: what do you mean tomato, you're a piece of shit. And what about you? says the turd, if you're a tomato, why do you act like a piece of shit? What a good joke; it always made her laugh. She didn't feel her body; it was motionless and cold. She thought there was a peaceful splendor in the air and she was part of it; she could go on like this for who knows how long, weeks, months, years, and it did not disturb her to think so. She was surrounded by peace. If she closed her eyes, the world was reduced to two hot eyelids that covered her like two loving hands. With their fine veil the eyelids separated Luisa from what remained of the sky. Her window, the city, and the whole world in the abyss of the sky. Only two thin, soft eyelids before the infinite. It's happiness, she thought, and it was her last thought. The breath still ran through its dark ways, but almost by chance. A bit of air passed in and lost itself in the body. Many seconds went by before the chest found the strength to breathe out, but the air continued to lose itself and almost nothing came out. Her body had no further need of air. The heart, too, barely throbbed from time to time. It was night when it stopped beating and Luisa's eyelids closed forever.

The young men shouted; the televisions blared and sang from a thousand apartments. The lights in her house were all lit; even the blue one in the bedroom diffused an illusion of coolness. Luisa's face was serene, sunk in repose.

They found her several days later, and two municipal employees took her away. The funeral and burial went according to the letter of her last wishes. Ten people took part in the ceremony, including Renata's husband and children; she cried the whole time. The apartment, however, was renovated, and for two months the residents of the building cursed the dust and work. At the end of October her niece Cristina went to live there.